TELLINGS FROM THE ETHERS

Edited by Gaone Koloka

Table of Contents

Tellings From The Ethers 1
Dedicated to you, | Basebi Betty 'Mmathipa' Mangwa. 2
PREFACE 3
CHAPTER 1 – PERSONAL ESSAYS 4
The Sick Healers 5
This House Is Not a Home 12
The Boy with a Golden Heart 15
Superheroes Are Real and I've Met Some 18
CHAPTER 2 - FICTION 21
Teenage Woes 22
Identity 35
CHAPTER 3 – AFRO-FUTURISM 45
Transition 46
Out of the Matrix 51
CHAPTER 4 – AFRO-MYTHOS, ADVENTURE AND FANTASY 57
Encounters with the Yellow Goddess 58
Of Flying Things 63
Images of a Nation's Consciousness 69
Images of a Nation's Consciousness: Part 2 72
Images of a Nation's Consciousness: Part 3 75
BONUS CHAPTER 79
Manuscripts and Broken Promises 80
EPILOGUE 84

PREFACE
CHAPTER 1 – PERSONAL ESSAYS

The Sick Healers
This House Is Not a Home
The Boy with a Golden Heart
Superheroes Are Real and I've Met Some

CHAPTER 2 - FICTION

Teenage Woes
Identity

CHAPTER 3 – AFRO-FUTURISM

Transition
Out of the Matrix

CHAPTER 4 – AFRO-MYTHOS, ADVENTURE AND FANTASY

Encounters with the Yellow Goddess
Of Flying Things
Images of a Nation's Consciousness
Images of a Nation's Consciousness: Part 2
Images of a Nation's Consciousness: Part 3

BONUS CHAPTER

Manuscripts and Broken Promises

EPILOGUE

Dedicated to you,

Basebi Betty 'Mmathipa' Mangwa.

May you continue to rest in eternal peace.

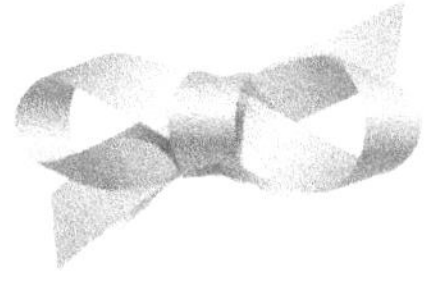

PREFACE

I am no longer trying to be 'cool'. My primary concern as of late is that of being myself. My heart is glowing. I now know who I am outside of what these two eyes can see. With this body of work, this revelation is apparent. Within this body of work lies the intricate details of how the pen and the keypad have assisted me in putting together words, from places where parts of me also needed to be fetched and put together into this entity I am currently.

• • ❧ • •

...AND THE TRAVELLER GIRDS himself, and sets his face toward the Morning, and goes his way.

W.E.B Du Bois

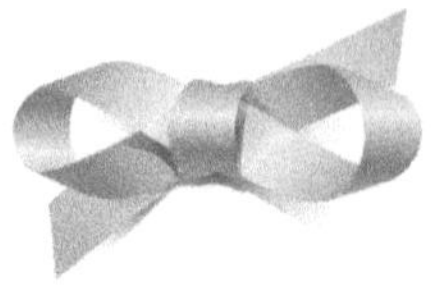

CHAPTER 1 – PERSONAL ESSAYS

When the bloodline is ready to transmutate, and this realization dawns on *you*, you'll begin to comprehend fully why you say and do things in a certain manner. Sometimes, no, most times, those things make sense only to you. If you're lucky, it'll be you and a few others you seem to really be close with.

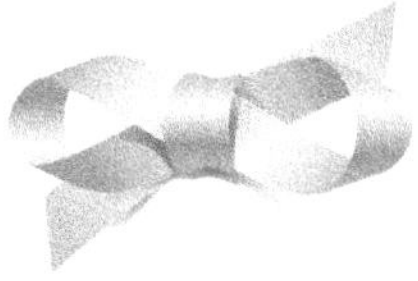

The Sick Healers

Growing up in the city with my little brother, our parents had moulded this life for us where we knew we were provided for-even when we were too young to fathom what that really meant. To be quite honest, what was etched into my brain was seeing our mother do all she can to provide for my brother and I. She still does. That energy she put in became somewhat of a sacrifice in the sense that, she spent most of her hours grinding for her kids. This meant that the various offices she laboured at saw more of her than her kids. Not to sound ungrateful but, this also might've played a part in terms of there being a disconnect between a child's early stages of development to their adult stage and a mother's comprehension of the little but significant details that go hand in hand with all of that. This shortfall would show its face in a not-so-pleasing manner at a later stage in life. I consciously and continuously saw her actions and efforts, and our dad was always at the beck and call of his two beloved boys. Or at least he tried. Rather, as an honouring to him, the best thing to say would be that he did his best under the circumstances.

The funny thing is our parents were together for as long as I can recall, but they did not live together. There would be days when *Pops*[1] would sleep at our house on some nights but that was on good days. As a kid, you see these things happening but it doesn't really click as to why they are happening. You are just content with the way things are because the way things are seems to work. It's also a *mind-fuck* when finding out why that was the case, deciding to keep it a secret thinking you're protecting the ones that matter to you the most or that you just solved a case, only to find out that everyone else around you, especially in the most intimate surrounding, already knew everything. Wouldn't I make an awesome detective! Let's not even go there because that's another story all on its own-one that deserves its own title and blank canvas.

It was one fateful night when things went south and what seemed to have been working for the longest time started to show cracks. The exact details are a bit sketchy but I was seventeen or eighteen at the time. My brother is five years younger than I am. If memory serves me right, mom and Pops came home from an outing that night. Pops had over-indulged. They were in the car outside the house while my bro and I were watching television. Fast forward, the two of them are having a heated argument-an argument so heated that Pops ended up smashing the windows and whatever he could get his hands on in the living room-where my brother and I were. Whether my brother understood what was really happening that night or not, only time will tell when it encourages him to garner enough strength to heal himself. And if memory doesn't serve me right, that just goes to show how traumatic the experience might have been because to be honest, I don't even have any recollection of where in the house my little brother was when the scene was playing itself out. What I do vividly recall though was pops, mom and I in *their* bedroom exchanging hurtful words and me conjuring up enough courage to stand in front of my mother and tell him to leave. This was to be the precursor to us moving from the city to our home village.

• • ❧ • •

IN LATE 2011, OUR MOTHER took us to our home village (Oodi[2]) for the long-term when gentrification was starting to *pop off*[3]. We used to travel back and forth between our city home and our home village during some weekends and especially during holidays. It was an epic experience-a rendezvous with our favourite relatives. Living there permanently was a totally different experience that took a while to get used to. It set up a bunch of interactions with relatives that allowed me to tap into learning more about my roots. I'll humbly admit that our home village had and still has something to show me and once I surrendered to what that might be an unfolding happened.

Throughout all the years we lived there, there were so many epiphanies for me that piggy-backed off of the fact that there were certain events that led all three of us to where we were. In the midst of all this, however, my bro would keep to himself and only interact with very few people. He would give hints as to why he does that but it took me some time to realize and understand what that actually meant-to realize that he was an *empath*. See, my brother is a great listener but I've also come to find that he seldom communicates how he really feels-that's even if he knows how to express how he really feels but I talk too much so even *that* took me a while to realize. When mom is out doing her thing, it would be my brother and I at home. I would talk and he would listen. He would listen and listen and listen even to my philosophical jargon that I just finished reading about on the internet or somewhere in a book.

One of the things Oodi had to show me was that I had to learn or relearn how to be a big brother. There would be this feeling of guilt within pertaining to how I wasn't the big brother my little brother needed. Writing this now, I still don't think I know what it means exactly to be a big brother. Or maybe perhaps it's because my little brother has found his own way of manoeuvring in his world as his own big brother. All I know is that I wish I had one-someone to talk to when I'm not talking to myself. Lol. Anyway, I remember that after this particular epiphany, he and I had a heart to heart as I felt like I owed him a huge apology for the characteristics that had lacked.

The interactions on my side were with various relatives in what seemed to be an investigation of some sort. Curiosity had gotten the best of me. It was raining family puzzles, epiphanies and revelations to the point where there were family issues that were revealed to me that blew my mind. The light came with the dark and I started to realize just how messed up our family was/is. So much bad blood that makes one ponder on some things, you know-a sick family that needs healing. Which family doesn't?!

Is it an African thing where the older generation is beefing among each other and expects the younger ones to follow suit by making it seem like the other party is the only one that is guilty of some crazy shit that happened in the past?

• • ❧ • •

IN OODI IS WHERE I also learnt how to forgive Pops for the stunt he pulled at our city home. As a side-note, it would probably be wise for me to mention the fact that we grew up in the Church. Both parents are Christians. Our mom would take us to church every Sunday. Bro would show his distaste for it and mom would rush to reprimand him to save face in front of her fellow church members. I tended to be more receptive to it, not because I knew what religion meant but because I wanted to see my mother happy. However, church took a backseat once I was old enough to make my own decision about whether to go or not. Eventually, I stopped going because religion has its people and to each his own. Going back to significant occurrences in Oodi, it became obvious why certain things relating to our family were kept in the dark and why *that* relative does not gel well with their parent or another relative or whatever. My grandmother would spill the beans and I felt like a tabloid journalist with exclusives continuously raining from the heavens like Manna. In all honesty, this was my student phase. As a student, the rabbit hole went deeper. Nine years after we moved to our home village, my brother was knee-deep within a very confusing phase of his life. Parents thought it was depression. It could've been both but it was a very dark time for him. Shit got real, real quick. It's also not unfitting to acknowledge that there were events that led to the phase he was in.

Cognizant of the fact that my little brother needed a *different* kind of help, after the psychologist gave him a clean bill of health, which didn't really help him with his situation, I decided to contact *spiritual healers* in our village and set up a consultation on my bro's request. Since religion had become a past life thing for me, this was how I became more open to other avenues of faith and was thus willing to assist my bro in the manner in which I did. After our mother found out, her first reaction was that of confusion as was my grandmother's and Pops' as well. These are the only people who knew about the "blasphemy" my bro and I had committed. I say "blasphemy" because none of them knew where we got the audacity to set up a consultation with spiritual healers in a family of proclaimed Christians. On my side there were and are still no regrets and from the consultation, there was a lot of truth that answered some of the questions my brother had. We also found out that all the symptoms he had during his dark phase were brought about by those that were part of his DNA but no longer living on this earth. This also meant that there was an initiation ceremony that had to take place because this was a *calling* and my little brother had to surrender to it. Something our grandmother and parents could not quite/did not want to comprehend.

The first irony is that at first, all the three people who knew of this ordeal denied that there was someone in the family who was no longer living but had had a similar calling to that of my brother-that everything we were told at the consultation was false and a means for the healers to rob us of our monies. Because Oodi still has something to show me, our grandmother's sister, who's a Christian as well but seems to still be in touch with her African Spirituality, and is basically our other grandmother, told my brother and I the truth about our lineage but we never told our mother, grandmother (who always has an ailment somewhere on her body but her doctor doesn't seem to know exactly what is wrong with her) or father about what we found out. Our grandmother once even told me that ancestral talk/veneration is against her church's laws but she has all these prophetic dreams about *weird* things and people she knows and those she doesn't know-*the second irony*. Our father still has to call a senior at his church to come and address my brother and me after the stunt we pulled.

At our home, there are only three of us, us and our mom. There's less tension that there was after what happened as our mother felt we had invited *bad energy* into our home. Both my mother's sons have this built up resentment as an aftermath. Truthfully, I've come across some meditation and more revelations that have helped me deal with that resentment-to understand that mother did what she did because she felt that she was doing the best thing to protect her children. She's probably still shocked about it. It's been slow progress but progress nonetheless for me but I cannot say the same for my little brother. Imagine feeling like your own mother is standing between you and your destiny. He's more reserved now more than ever, especially towards my mother and I find myself caught in between trying to retain the peace and harmony in our home, acting as a low-level diplomat who's in way over his head. That has not stopped me from trying though. Here I am trying to balance emotions of these two people that I love and sacrificing myself in the process. That also does not negate the fact that this relationship between mother and son is now estranged. It looks like our mother is drowning herself in more work as a coping mechanism. On the days that my brother does come out of his room, I see him close each and every door behind him every chance he gets, sometimes unnecessarily. This is so frequent that one time that happened, something clicked in me, perhaps another revelation/ epiphany that provided a much needed part of an explanation that showed how reserved internally he had become. So I would observe and observe and therefore became fascinated by how self-betraying human behaviour was/is. I have even thought about telling him that he needs to learn *the art of how to talk to people when you don't want to talk to people* for all our sakes. It remains a thought thus far.

My grandmother still confides in me about her dreams, the pains on her body, how they keep moving to different parts, how the pain-killer tablets nor the other prescribed pills aren't effective enough in alleviating the pain. I listen because people appreciate being listened to and also because I love her regardless of the decisions she makes or things she says that tend to border on *defeatism* or *pessimism*. All the sickness has become normalized and I do not think that is the best way to address it because after a while, it sets up shelter and doesn't budge; it feels entitled. What I think is that finding the root cause of it and dealing with it goes a longer way.

How the rest of this story will unfold, we'll see. But the *third* and biggest irony of it all is when it's a family of healers but everyone is sick!

• • ❦ • •

1. AN INFORMAL TERM for a dad/father.

2. A village in the Kgatleng District of Botswana. It is located 20 km north-east of Gaborone (Botswana's capital city).

3. An informal term referring to the beginning of the peak of a specific event.

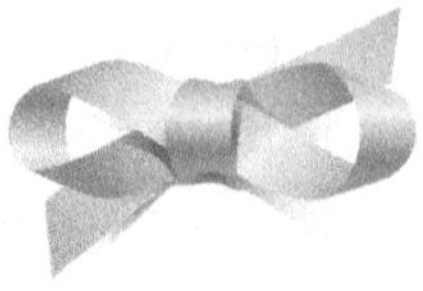

This House Is Not a Home

Stranded in a village I thought was home but wasn't because even though it had received me and mine well, its residents chose to betray the intentions it had for us. I am tired. Tired of living in a place where people pretend to care about each other. Neighbours greet each other with fake smiles and the minute their backs are turned, they cannot wait to gossip to them to an ally. By the way, allies are important in this village, *apparently*—someone willing to be a participant in your battle with someone else when the time is right-sometimes unknowingly. There's no loyalty. I do not think there is true friendship either. You keep the ally close enough to assist you in the battle(s) you foresee coming. Sun Tzu must have alluded to this somewhere in *The Art of War*, right?! As if they read and studied the book...

I am part of a family that wanted peace so badly that they resorted to losing a great part of who they are to acquire it. Can you blame me for not wanting a piece of that peace? Is it human nature to want so much to belong to a group or community, to the extent that we're willing to do anything, even going against our common sense, our own personal values and things we regard to be of utmost importance to us—just to fit in?

Before moving permanently to Oodi, most of my family lived where I was born, Selebi Phikwe* but I cannot recall any experiences from there. The ones I mostly recall are of the city of Gaborone*, where my younger brother and I grew up till we relocated to this not-so-homey place back in 2011—The most ideal place at the time for our mother to build us a home because she had had enough of working tirelessly with nothing much to show for it but rental receipts. At the moment this essay was being written, it was written from inside the beautiful home that our mother has provided for us and it has become a safe haven from what is out *there*.

When things get too much to handle in Oodi, my grandmother reminisces about all the good memories etched into her being from the good ol' days in Phikwe. Perhaps also, those are the days her family used to get along. Those days are dead and gone now. I get why she's always more than welcoming to take a trip to where her idea of a utopia is—Even if it's just for a week or two. If memory serves me right, my mother once alluded to her older child that she raised my younger brother and I away from our home village to keep us away from its *negative vibration*—For her sanity as well.

Remember all those European medieval movies about witches being hunted down and burnt at the stake? See, Botswana has also been bitten by the Westernization bug. And boy have we owned our illness! But then again, what is the best thing to do when the only thing you can recall before the bug bit is the magnificent aesthetics of the bug when it first came within your line of sight? Isn't a cultural exchange meant to be exactly that-a cultural exchange? Doesn't it become something else when the scales are tipped in favour of one side? My heart bled when I heard such stories from my grandmother about those in my lineage that came before me. Forgiveness seems like a steep mountain climb from where I'm standing.

At one point I wanted to leave this place indefinitely but my extended family, or at least the ones I know, and some ancestors are buried here. That is what made me think twice about it. As a matter of fact, it appears that most of my relatives here, if given the chance, would take the first bus out of here-anywhere but here. My mom once said to me that when she passes and my brother and I want to relocate to some other place, she gives us her blessing to do so. My mom's house is a home but I cannot say the same about the house that is this place I now reside in. However, as I've written before, somewhere else, there are lessons that Oodi wants to teach me and I may not be able to permanently relocate till it has taught all its lessons in full to its satisfaction! I can only pray that when the time comes, my heart will have reached a point where it rejoices because it is now as light as the feather it's being measured against on *the* scale.

• • ❧ • •

*SELEBI-PHIKWE IS A mining town located in the Central District of Botswana.

*Gaborone is the capital city of Botswana.

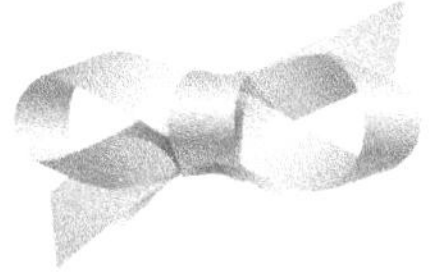

The Boy with a Golden Heart

The boy with a golden heart was raised by his aunt together with his younger brothers and sisters. He has an older brother but they aren't that close. Our friendship goes back as far as I can remember. Every holiday, our family would traverse from our dwelling place in the city to our home village which happened to be his as well. Our families' houses were in close proximity to each other metaphorically and literally speaking, so every chance we got, my younger brother and I would go over to theirs and it would be a fun rendezvous with him and his siblings. He is three years my senior but I'm older than all his younger siblings. This routine would be the reason why this boy and I would become best friends.

When we were younger, I had no idea that his aunt didn't get along with most of her family. I doubt he did too. When we were younger, I had no idea that most of the older generation in *my* own family didn't get along with each other. As we grew older and began to comprehend a few things about our families, I found myself to be a reflection of the boy with a golden heart.

Our elders are complaining. They say that they do not understand this young generation but this young generation comes from them—in more ways than one. This young generation is a reflection of something internal they do not understand about themselves—or *choose not to* understand about themselves. It remains hidden deep within but haunts them through their offspring. The young ones do not want to go to their home villages. They sense that something is wrong. There's some bullshit going on over there. There's *beef* amongst the elders—or something else. Either way all of it is of a low frequency. Negative vibes, they say and subconsciously, sometimes consciously as well, they avoid that as much as possible. It's just not them.

He's all grown up now—an adult. But I still refer to him as *the boy* because he's truly a child at heart. Pure in his intentions and to be honest I wish for the shortfall of that which tries to taint this purity. Age-wise he hasn't been an adult for a long time but maturity sometimes says something else and speaks the wisest. So he spends most of what has been his adult-life thus far doing his best to bring his family together at any cost. His cause is a noble one. To say noble sounds like an insult but I use that to describe the statue of his character and therefore his deeds.

• • ❧ • •

ONE NIGHT, HE COMES to my mother's house to lament and ask for her assistance as an elder because he just knocked off from work but finds her absent, so I find myself standing in for my mother. It's ok because he's practically family—one of my besties. As he speaks, I feel the pain coming through his utterings. He speaks the night away and tells me how he dislikes the fact that whatever issues the older generation has seem to be spilling onto the younger ones and something needs to be done to circumvent that, as well as the importance of this being done urgently. His golden heart is a blessing and a curse and as I listen to him I get the feeling that this is something he absolutely has to carry to fruition or else the greatest part of him will cease to exist.

It takes about a year but finally, the boy with a golden heart invites me to the first family gathering in a long time—possibly the most peaceful since his childhood. I am honored and inspired. Words cannot begin to describe how I'm feeling when I see it all playing out. The most interesting thing is that there are those that admit that they've been yearning for a gathering of this sort but didn't know how to go about it.

As we sit next to a bonfire that night of the gathering, I do my best to conjure up the most heartfelt statement acknowledging his efforts. His aunt that raised him comes but doesn't stay long—his older brother too. He's still grateful they did. He would've preferred it if more had come but this is a good start. Looking at each other, we smile as if to say we cannot wait for the next one—He a tad more than I. What a way to end the year!

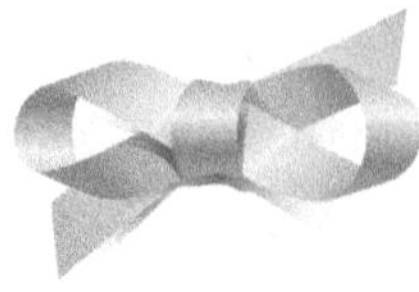

Superheroes Are Real and I've Met Some

MP and I are indoors, doing this and that. All of a sudden we hear high-pitched voices shouting our names from the outside. He looks through the open curtain and it's our little cousins here to visit. Rising up from the chair at my study table, I follow my little bro's lead. There's something I'm busy with but can't help but feel inconsiderate for wanting to send them back to our granny's house instantaneously. At that moment, there's an internal voice that asks me if this will be the norm in my own home with my partner and *our* kids— a moment of silence for this short but effective burst of shame.

As MP rushes to open the gate for them, I keep wondering how this scenario is going to work out. Luckily, my bro is great with kids so *I* am in good hands. Just as expected, he plays his role and plays it well— my hero! There's something mindboggling to me about the way these kids behave. They seem excited to see *both* of us. I don't have any exciting activities planned for them and nothing is coming to mind at this moment but that doesn't seem to bother them. They are here to spend time with *us* and that's what they care mostly about. Again, MP leads and I follow. As I write this piece, I realize that if I were to come face to face with my *child-self* then, I probably wouldn't have known how to go about addressing him— just like I don't know how to go about addressing my little cousins when it matters the most. It's almost night time and time for them to head back to granny's house. I have to admit though, I'm a little glad that the day is over but what has transpired is a bit concerning for me.

I've always been soft-spoken for as far back as I can remember especially towards strangers/people I'm not really familiar with. Even with people I'm close with, it comes and goes for fear of oversharing. Even at this current point in my short life, I have embarked on a pursuit to figure out why I have such a hard time expressing myself in a normal conversation— why it's most times difficult for me to speak my thoughts, especially to close friends and family. Perhaps there's trauma attached to it. If so then all the darkness must come forth and embrace the light. The irony is that when I'm on stage performing a spoken-word piece or song my best friend and I has recorded, I feel as if it's someone totally different. I have not the words to describe the experience further.

Our family is relatively large. Which African family isn't?! Lol! We have quite a lot of cousins and most of the younger ones love visiting my bro and me. To be honest, I thought they came here for MP till he told me that every time they visited, they would ask where I am. I'd be lying if I said I haven't noticed from since I was conscious of my surroundings that children have *some* affinity towards me— whether they know me or not. For some reason, I've become oblivious to this fact and subconsciously keep trying to push them away but to no avail.

These little cousins of ours have made it a ritual to visit my brother and me. They assist me with my articulation and how I deliver what I have to say. They teach me how to be patient with others and more importantly, with myself, to have fun, how to actually be present in the moment, as well as not to forget my *child-self* as I grow up and learn the dos and don'ts of *adulting*. As if I have a choice! I have become them in order to find myself. These kids unknowingly *or* knowingly gave me a riddle to solve and the weird thing is they are helping me solve it. One might even go further to say these kids *are* the riddle. They are the real superheroes and they incessantly save me from myself. For that, I am glad I met them and will forever be grateful for their rescue mission regardless of whether I feel I deserve it or not.

I LOOK IN THE MIRROR and see these kids,
Every dialog with them,
Is a dialog with expression in its purest form.

There are many superheroes and Superman is surely one of the ones that stand out. Superman uses his physical strength to move a mountain but your voice can move multiple mountains with minimum effort. Therefore, use it. And use it well.

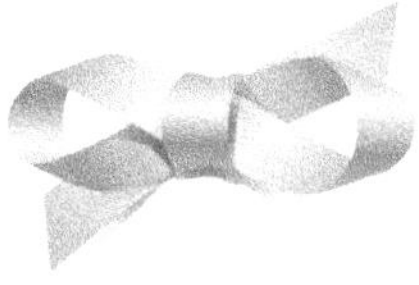

CHAPTER 2 - FICTION

...Trying so hard to be different that we forget to be ourselves. Trying so hard to be different that we forget how to be ourselves... May we not drown in the identities of others while there's a raft we came to these waters with tied indefinitely to the most authentic part of ourselves.

Teenage Woes

Up until junior high school, Lesedi would not have imagined himself doing the whole *dating* thing. He was a nerdy, shy guy who was more concerned with whatever else nerdy teenage boys are concerned with during that adolescent phase.

Form 2/grade 9 was when he started dating. This girl showed interest in him and she was cute so hey, why not. A beautiful name, she had; Wada. Unfortunately, Lesedi wasn't the only one who took affection to Wada. A guy he had met before from the adjacent classroom shared this affection as well. To top it all off, they shared the same name. He decided to do something about it-to show them that he didn't like the fact that Wada wasn't with him instead. So he turned into a bully. He started bullying his less mentally experienced and less muscular-bodied nemesis and it worked because after three days the "relationship" ended. What a pity. Apparently, the girl was heavily invested into the relationship that after the breakup, she went through a phase where she lost faith in love. After three days? Imagine! Lesedi being the soft-spoken person that he is, felt that all the drama was not worth it. Wada's best friend despised Lesedi for a while but eventually let it go. What else could she have done? She saw Lesedi frequently-she was his best friend's neighbor. Wada never knew the real reason for the breakup lest she come to the conclusion that her boyfriend was a coward that failed to fight for what should follow after a stable foundation is laid. Is it really that deep? After that stint, there was the girl from his class. He told himself that it wasn't her fault, that it was all new to him and that he wasn't ready for her.

Senior high school was a totally different ballgame for Lesedi. He'd gained some experience, had a bit more self-confidence and self-esteem to carry him further. Back in his home village, before schools opened, he had had an opportunity to kiss a girl he liked under the rain. Just like in the movies. He couldn't sleep for a while that night, reminiscing over the experience.

Lesedi and all of his closest friends were lucky enough to get accepted to the same Senior high school, Goodhope Senior Secondary school. In Botswana, primary, junior high school and senior high school have three terms per year divided into about three academic months with the remaining three months taken by a four week school holiday per term. Form 5/grade 12 is the year the final exams, being the *Botswana General Certificate for Secondary Education* (BGCSE) exams, are written towards the end of the year in preparation for the next stage in education, tertiary/varsity.

First term of form 5 is usually dedicated to sports especially athletics and various track events. There was this girl who was an athlete *and cute*, Thabang. Of course she caught Lesedi's eye and he did try his luck a couple of times but got turned down all those times. One time he decided to try a different approach, to join the athletics team she was a part of. While still in *the pursuit of cute Thabang*, Lesedi often got Intel about her from her bestie, Michele, who happened to be in the same class as one of his boys within the same block as the classroom Lesedi was in. Her bestie was one of the popular cool girls in school-arguably the coolest. She did all that was in her power to try and help him score points with Thabang but to no avail. None of Lesedi's hommies approved of such a crush nor the tactics used to try and win this girl over. They thought her too *tomboy-ish* for their *liking*. Obviously, that did not stop him because he *always* went after what he wanted. The funny thing is, she recognized and acknowledged Lesedi's efforts but still wasn't *budging*. Thabang was also quite friendly but badass at the same time and unfortunately for Lesedi, she *friendzoned* him, even after he joined the athletics team for her "love and affection." Lol! Eventually that crush died out.

That was the last time Lesedi tried his luck and one time while introspecting he realized that joining the athletics team had its benefits and thus was actually a cool idea. They had travelled around Botswana but he was more of a backbencher than an actual partaker. He had been there for one reason and one reason only-to get *his* Thabang. The other consolation was the team trips. There would be all kinds of silly games being played on the bus, the wins and losses, the talent from the school team and the other teams from the same region as theirs and he made a couple of new friends.

During the second term one of Lesedi's best friends, Kaelo, got into a relationship with one of the prettiest girls in her class. He adored her. She had two girl best friends and Lesedi found himself *vibing* with one of them. However, things did not work out between them and Lesedi felt it wasn't right to continue contact with his bestie's ex's bestie, so he cut all communication with her. They say that everything happens for a reason-a saying that consoled Lesedi for a while after another girl he liked sometime during the first term dumped him via a text on his birthday.

In the latter part of second term of form 5, Lesedi fell in *like* with a girl that was his junior (form 4) and they dated briefly. Samantha was her name. As much as we think we're grown during our teenage years as we approach our twenties, life sometimes humbles us, shows us that everything happens gradually. Peer pressure is a stage most if not all of us pass through and as foolish as it may seem, even your friends mocking your relationship can have an effect on its outcome regardless of whether they do it as a harmless joke or otherwise. Some of Lesedi's friends used to mock him about how he and his girl looked alike-that he was dating his sister. He got turned off and broke up with her. Such pettiness!

IT WAS THE FINAL TERM of form 5, the last term of Lesedi's final senior school year and exams were approaching. Most of his teachers had little hope in their class due to the previous test marks prior to the final BGCSE exams. Most of the class was discouraged for a while but the strongest classmates somehow found a way to reassure the rest of their capabilities.

After calling it quits with trying to get Thabang into his life, Lesedi stayed in contact with her bestie Michele throughout the rest of that year. They started getting closer and talking more from the beginning of the third term. They got so close that Lesedi developed a crush for her but did not act on it for a while. As time went by, he developed some feelings for her. She had another bestie who happened to be one of my classmates. She knew Lesedi liked Michele and even put in a good word for him plenty of times. It worked and to make it *official*, he invited Michele over to his mother's house in her absence, of course-must be a high school thing. She agreed, came over, he made pasta and canned beef, one of the very few things he knew how to make. She acknowledged his efforts and to probably stroke his ego, she told him that the meal combination was one of her favorites. Lesedi played Drake's *Shut It Down* on his mother's radio, put it on replay and they danced over the song-a song that became their theme song. The song definitely set the mood and before they knew it, their lips were interlocked for a while before they realized that it was time for her to go home. Lesedi's mom was about to knock off and he did not want his mom to find her house in the state it was in, so they snapped back into reality and he walked her to the bus stop, making sure she got the transport she needed to get home. *He* walked back home ecstatic with butterflies in his stomach!

Michele and Lesedi dated for two months and it happened that those were also the last left of senior school. In the last month of their relo, they'd have conversations inside one of the empty classrooms, as this was during exam time and most students were studying at home.

She would ask him questions about how sure he was that this *thing* between them wasn't infatuation. He really liked this girl and some would've argued that it was damn near "love". So her asking him such questions confused him a lot. He actually tried to convince her that his feelings towards her were authentic and genuine but that seemed to have a short-term effect on her. Lesedi would also hear rumors that she was *lowkey* dating another guy in the same school but dismissed the rumors immediately. His beloved wouldn't do that to him, would she? Of course she wouldn't!

A week after the final BGCSE exam paper was written and ex-candidates were no-longer Goodhope students, Michele sent Lesedi a text saying that she loved him but she needed a "break". That was the last time they talked. A few years later, he would spot her for the first time after their split. She was coming from school, him from an internship job. They were walking towards each other in opposite directions but he looked away before she could notice him.

There was this other girl, Amanda. She was in the same class as Lesedi's ex-girlfriend, Michele. This girl would later use him to get back at one of his closest friends and fellow crew members for whatever *he* did to her.

• • ❦ • •

LESEDI'S BOY, KAELO was turning eighteen and he had thrown an intimate house party at his house in Phase 4 to celebrate. Lesedi arrived there at some time past seven at night with their other homie, Steve, because they lived near to each other. Where they lived was also of walking distance to Kaelo's crib. Kaelo had made a strong alcoholic concoction that had Lesedi *faded* within a few minutes of arrival. Amanda arrived a while later. She and Lesedi then went to chill and talk by a spot just outside Kaelo's crib. This would be the only thing Lesedi would remember as well as Amanda asking, "Why don't you kiss me, then?" as he had been heavily intoxicated at that point. He later found out from his hommies that he had made out with Amanda on frequent occasions during the party but couldn't recall any of this.

On the night, Amanda had not had a lot to drink, or she could handle her liquor. She had taken pictures of her and Lesedi making out and posted them on Facebook for everyone to see-actually, so that one of Lesedi's closest friends, who it turns out, was his ex, could see them. Lesedi asked her to get rid of the pics from Fb. She refused initially but eventually did-after they had done the damage she wanted them to do. That caused a huge rift between Lesedi and his homie. Lesedi had been caught in between whatever game they were playing. He tried to plead his innocence to his boy but sadly ended up losing one of his closest. That was the last time Lesedi saw Amanda in person.

Samantha and Lesedi remained friends after their breakup and as a belated birthday present, she came to his mom's house in Block 8 and suggested they go and buy a bottle of Gin at the nearest liquor store to celebrate-in her absence of course. To our parents, we only drink alcohol after we turn the legal age of eighteen. To be quite honest, to all African parents reading this, we don't even drink at all till we're twenty one years old! This was later in the month of April. Lesedi's birthday had been on the 18th of the same month. All this happened post senior school while he was still waiting for his final form 5 results. This is usually a three to four months waiting period after exams for the ex-candidates.

Samantha had brought her female friend along and they got introduced to each other-the start of what was to be a very fruitful friendship. At this point, Lesedi was single. Ready to mingle was the norm. They got home from the liquor store and unfortunately the bottle slipped from the unstable table they put it on, fell to the ground and broke before they could open it-an unforeseen libation for all the lost ones. Lesedi's excitement and anticipation for tasting raw hard liquor for the first time had been short-lived but of course, Sam and her buddy didn't know that. They all looked at the bottle like "what a loss!"

All that was left was to have a "naked" conversation and converse they did.

Samantha's friend, Larona came off as mysterious and therefore quite interesting to Lesedi although she was reserved on that day-understandably so. As the Tuesday sun was setting, he took them halfway to the bus stop and immediately when he got home, got onto Facebook and sent Larona a friend request. She accepted his request and that is how the two became friends. His intention was not to date her at all. As months went by, they became closer and even hung out a couple of times. It wasn't until the next year around November that the two decided to give it a shot-a year and some months after they had first met. They were both excited about it since they had gotten pretty close and none could deny any longer that there was chemistry between them. This was however short-lived as she decided to break off the relo a few weeks later much to Lesedi's confusion. He had done all he could to be the best boyfriend he could and for the longest time, he hadn't a clue as to the actual reason for the break up but of course a few hypotheses were conjured up. The first one being the tattoo of his ex she had seen on their first date (which she was clearly distraught about). The second possibly being that she was still dealing with some things emotionally and simply wasn't ready for a relationship but thought she was. Lesedi was obviously hurt by the ordeal having been a softy that was damn near in love with Larona and didn't hide it. He was a casualty and thus feelings of resentment towards her built up that a few months later when he was at UB visiting and chilling with some of his hommies, he saw her from a distance and wanted to tell her where to get off. His best friend Kaelo, however, stopped him and told him to stop being bitter. From that day on, he decided to dig deep within himself and let go of the grudge he held against her-to deal with the feelings he obviously still had for her. It was none of her business anyway. She had her own issues to deal with.

AT THE BEGINNING OF the year during the post-final exam waiting period, Kaelo and Lesedi decided to volunteer as Guidance and Counseling teaching assistants at the same senior high school they went to-Goodhope Senior School. One major thing about Lesedi was that he was such a lover that whenever he got into a relationship, he would go all in without holding back-no matter the consequences. Facebook being the *weird* matchmaker that it is connected Lesedi with Karabo, one of the students from one of the form 5 classes he had been teaching. The rest is history as they say.

Lesedi and Kaelo were part of a crew of aspiring producers and rappers that was formulated in the early weeks of form 4. All this they were juggling while trying not to lose sight of the fact that they were in senior school and focus was imperative at this stage in their lives. They also had their fair share of dating and relos to add onto all of that. These two friends would grab any opportunity to perform on stage at any event no matter how small it was. So one weekend they got a gig to perform at a talent show in Maru-a-Pula school (MAP). To Lesedi's surprise, Karabo came to the gig to see their performance. It was an amazing night. They shared the stage with one of Botswana's biggest Motswako* artists, *Dramaboi* at the time he was coming up. After the show, Lesedi and Karabo made out but unfortunately it was late, the cab guy was impatient and the two *superstars* left in a rush leaving Karabo there with *her* bestie. This was the kiss that made it official. They were now officially an item.

Earlier that day, Lesedi had bumped into Miley-one of his new-found friends. They had been *Facebook friends* for a little while. She was from a tennis game by the court at the venue he and his bestie were to perform at. They exchanged numbers. Talking continuously via Fb*, texts and calls, they got so close that they would tell each other *everything* about each other. A level of comfort on another level but not on the level of more than friends as Lesedi was in a relationship. This was in the early weeks of Lesedi and Karabo's relo but that doesn't make it right. Clearly he was still not mature enough to comprehend that there are other forms of cheating besides physical and he was knee-deep within it. This is evident in the fact that he allowed things to get out of hand that he developed feelings for Miley but because he was a softy, felt guilty about the heavy flirting and thus confessed his *sins* to Karabo. After his confession, Karabo decided to also take the opportunity to confess hers. She told him how on the night of their MAP performance, she had made out with some other guy after he and Kaelo left the venue in a rush. Saddened by this confession, he however convinced himself that he did not have the right to feel that way as it suddenly dawned on him that he had *technically* cheated as well. Crazy as it may sound, his confession led to their first breakup. Karabo called it all off and guess what, Lesedi couldn't wait to tell his friend Miley all about it.

Having been *touched* by the breakup, Lesedi made an impulsive decision to make a move on Miley. She surprisingly agreed and they made it "official"-over a phone call. The same day his girl broke up with him, he and Miley was now an item. Talk about heavy rebounding. Funny thing is, a few days later, his ex-girl decided to give him another chance and he didn't hesitate going back to her. By then Lesedi and Karabo were about three months into their relo excluding the breakup period that lasted only a few days. This, of course, devastated Miley-understandable. He had played with her emotions and that was a cowardly move on his part. As a result, he lost a good friend. For the longest time, she hated his guts but Lesedi somehow felt like she was overreacting not knowing how much damage he had done. She had trusted him and he threw it back in her face-with no remorse even. It took a while for him to conjure up enough strength to apologize to her but eventually he did. She clearly had found her own way to deal with it but it definitely brought some peace to Lesedi.

To celebrate four months of their relo, Lesedi decided to get a permanent mark on his body that represented his *love* for his girl.

Their relo was one of the genuine ones for Lesedi that lasted a good nine months where he got a chance to experience the reciprocation of the love and affection he always gave. At the tattoo parlor, one has to sign an agreement before the artist does their thing and one has to be *eighteen* years or above. Lesedi was *eighteen* but Karabo was *sixteen* and thus didn't "qualify" for a tattoo. So he decided to surprise her. Surprised, she was. Lesedi had always heard stories about people doing dumb things in relationships in the name of love like getting tattoos in honor of their partner and later regretting it when things go south. That didn't stop him though. The only thing going south would be him when he goes and asks for his girl's hand in marriage from her Uncles in Durban. So he went and got the tattoo without a second thought. The tattoo artist even warned him against it as if he could read his mind asking what the tattoo meant. Slick talk got Lesedi through the interrogation.

Things were going smoothly till around the month prior to the one leading up to their next breakup. Lesedi and Karabo had just made it to their ninth month together but Lesedi felt like there had been a communication breakdown the past couple of weeks. The *disconnect* was so intense that he thought about cheating. The irony is that he then sent Karabo a detailed breakup text and she replied with an "ok", nothing more. A few days before he sent the text, a female friend, Pamela, had visited him at his mom's house-once again, in her absence. His intention was to sleep with her. They only however, got to *first base* (kissing)-a horny virgin, Lesedi seemed to be. Fortunately for Lesedi, Pamela felt she wasn't ready as she had also never engaged in coitus before so first base it was. Lesedi's guilt brought about by this ordeal probably was the other reason he was *for* the breakup. Why he didn't ask for a link up so they could talk about it, perhaps he chose the easier option. Perhaps even a *better* one for *her* from her reply. It seemed like neither of them wanted to fight for the nine months of memories they had made. That was in February-valentine's week. That was it. Lesedi cried his ass off the following days although he made the move even calling his besties to cry to them about it. Fortunately, they got him through the rough patch. He then decided to take an indefinite hiatus from dating.

• • ꕥ • •

A FEW MONTHS PASSED and although Lesedi was in a good space mentally and emotionally, he hadn't a clue that he was still recovering from two consecutive breakups that had taken a lot out of him. Sometime in the first half of the next year, he started dating Kefilwe. An amazing girl he had seen and taken an interest in while he and his bestie Kaelo had been volunteering at their previous school, Goodhope two years earlier. The conversation started on Fb. No surprises there. Frequent flirting was their daily bread. See, Lesedi was a natural flirt. He'd find himself doing it as a reflex action-a blessing and a curse. Naturally, they agreed to try things out. About a month down the line, he felt like he was playing with Kefilwe's emotions as he felt absolutely nothing other than feelings of friendship for her. Lesedi confided in his other bestie, Leungo, about it and Leungo put it down bluntly that Lesedi hadn't had enough time to himself to recover from his past relos. Leungo gave great advice most of the time and this was clearly one of those times. A breakup was imminent and she understood. Lesedi felt like he should've stuck around for a while longer to see if anything develops but felt guilty being in a relo with someone he regarded as a friend and nothing more. Lesedi and Kefilwe remained friends although no longer as close and he still held her in high regard for the amazing soul that she was.

Deciding again, to take another break from relos, it was a couple of months of solitude before Lesedi and his ex-girl, Karabo started getting friendly again on Fb and WhatsApp. Eventually, they agreed that they missed each other and mistakenly got back together. This was sometime towards the end of that same year he had that thing with

Kefilwe. It wasn't long till one morning when Lesedi was just about to send his beloved a "good morning" text via WhatsApp and got a surprise when he took a glimpse of her profile pic/DP. It was an image of a heart that had lost its ability to feel. He immediately asked her about it and turns out the image meant what he thought it meant. She ended the relo but this time he didn't cry for her. She had her reasons but Lesedi had no time for them. He accepted it as he felt like it was a bunch of weight being lifted off his shoulders from something that was being forced. One day, while he was looking through their Fb inboxes, he realized that he was into the relo slightly more than Karabo was and perhaps the WhatsApp breakup was revenge or payback of some sort from her side. Sounds kind of far-fetched, right? Either way, that was the last time they ever spoke. One time Lesedi found an inbox from her asking if he still had the tattoo of her but he never responded.

The last breakup between Lesedi and Karabo took place while he was in varsity sometime after he turned twenty. After it happened, he decided to focus on his studies and that was evident in his marks. He breezed through varsity and in the last year met a beautiful girl who was taking a short-course on the same campus where he was attending classes. They became study partners. Nomvuyo was attending a Networking course and one of the modules in Lesedi's course was Networking. Nomvuyo completed her short-course with a distinction and on the night of Lesedi's graduation, they went on a date to celebrate their milestones. They would go to the same place they went for their first date for five years in a row till the place had to close down due to financial losses. They therefore had to find a new place to call their *own*.

One day, while at the park with his lady filled with gratitude, Lesedi had an epiphany that even though his teenage years seemed like a mess, his experiences had shaped him into the adult he was now- A lover who was never afraid to love but didn't know how and it now all made sense.

The alarm went off at the usual time of 4:44am. As Lesedi woke up to turn the alarm off, he realized that he had been deep within a dream that had taken place on the longest night of the year during the winter solstice. Astonished by the vividness of the dream filled with people he'd never seen before and places he'd never been to, he sat on his bed for a good five minutes to soak it all in before his mother's voice brought him back to earth. He couldn't wait to tell his friends about the dream as he got up from his bed to prepare for another teenager's affair at senior school.

• • ❧ • •

*MOTSWAKO IS A SOUTHERN African genre of hip hop popular in Botswana and South Africa.

*Fb is an informal shortened term for Facebook.

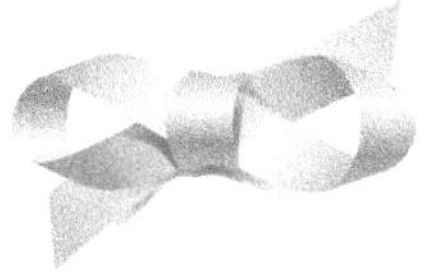

Identity

Kgosi[1] grew up in his home village of Oodi[2]. He attended his primary and high school there. Most of his extended family lived there as well and he was brought up by his community acting as an extension of his mother's phenomenal work. Having been raised in this type of environment, Kgosi was a relatively well-mannered boy, respected his elders and grew up secure and grounded in who he was especially having spent most of his life in a village, living a life that most city dwellers might call "*simple*".

Parents want to see their children excel where they could not and thus always strive to provide whatever is needed for this to happen. Kgosi's mother had only one child and had worked extremely hard to make sure that her son got the best education, especially since she finished school at Grade 12/form 5 and never got the opportunity to go to varsity. In the last year of senior school, which ends with form 5 in Botswana, mother made sure that she gave her son the necessary assistance he needed to garner enough points from the *Botswana General Certificate of Secondary Education* (BGCSE) exams that usually start around October, to get him into varsity. She stayed up with him during the nights leading up to the exams revising past papers and just being the anchor he needed to boost his confidence and motivate him enough to improve his self-belief that he could actually ace the exams with flying colors.

Another person who was very vital in assisting Kgosi with his preparations was his long-time best friend, Masego[3]-someone she had known since primary. They were from the same village and their mothers were neighbors and best friends as well. On weekends, they would go and fetch firewood together for cooking and bathing and would always get in trouble for coming home late, explaining that they lost track of time when they took a detour to the river side on their way back. As the years passed, they became even closer. Their closeness was often confused for that of a couple that was dating and in love-a difference that could only be understood by those that were lucky enough to be a part of their intimate space.

In the final year of senior school, form 5, Kgosi and Masego started dating to the surprise of a very few people-something that happened organically. Naledi Senior Secondary School (Naledi High[4]) had a reputation for being one of the best schools in Botswana and was looking to retain its number 1 spot from the BGCSE results of the previous year. This also added to the determination of both Kgosi and Masego to perform like the stars that the school was named after in the final exams. It also put some pressure on them and the rest of the students as well but it wasn't something they could not handle. They would go to the National library after school every day to go and study.

It is not surprising that both Kgosi and Masego got 48 points each in their final BGCSE/form 5 exams. This is the highest number of points a candidate can get based off of six subjects. This means that they got six A* from six subjects and one A* is eight points. They were a part of the top five national achievers. This was a feat that very few students from Oodi had achieved prior to them. Their parents, including the community that raised them, were filled with so much joy when the results came out that one of the community members donated a cow that was to be slaughtered as part of the celebration.

These two were really in sync with each other. They had both applied to one of the prestigious tertiary schools in Botswana, Botswana Accountancy College (BAC) for a Business Management course, not because they wanted to go where the other went but because they had both had a passion for business that stemmed from seeing their mothers from a young age partake in various business endeavors to make life easier for them-something they found fascinating. Being part of the top achievers, the Department of Tertiary Education and Funding (DTEF) was eagerly willing to sponsor them for any course they wanted. Having also the opportunity to study abroad, they had quite a lot of options but they however, both turned the opportunity down as they felt the need to empower kids who were from rural areas and felt like this achievement was too big for them to aim for.

• • ❧ • •

BAC HAS CAMPUSES IN Francistown[5] and Gaborone[6] and the course they applied for was present at both. They applied to the Gaborone campus and got accepted. This meant that they either had to commute to the Gaborone campus every day from Oodi or move to Gaborone, stay on campus and if they could not stay on campus, look for an affordable place to rent near the campus.

Kgosi and Masego managed to find space on campus and therefore they relocated from Oodi a week before classes were set to begin so as to settle in. It wasn't their first time in Gabs[7] but it *was* their first time living in Gabs so everything was kind of new to them-a new way of life. City lights can be blinding-something their parents gave them advice about before they left, trusting that their kin will not get swallowed up by the fast-flowing stream of Gabs' waters.

A week after tertiary school was officially underway, the BAC Student Representative Council's (SRC) entertainment Minister planned a *fresher's ball*[8] to welcome the first years to their varsity experience at the school. The event was a success but something had happened that would be the precursor to Kgosi's change in behavior and character. He had had his first taste of alcohol, in this case being hard liquor, vodka. He got so drunk that he started to *make out* with different girls at the event right in front of his girlfriend, Masego. The next day, he went to her room to ask for forgiveness, blaming the alcohol for his actions and she forgave him.

Business Management seemed like a course that Kgosi and Masego would cruise though with much ease. The first year went by with no issues. During the second semester of the second year, Kgosi started hanging out with the wrong crowd-the popular guys because he too wanted to be popular. He started giving Masego less and less of his attention but Masego attributed this to the pressure of the semester's upcoming final exams. At the end of the semester, Kgosi's marks had slightly declined from those of the previous semester. When Masego asked him the reason for this, he blatantly lied and told her that the course was starting to get tougher. She accepted his reason but something inside told her that there is more to it than just the course getting tougher. She let it go.

During the third year, Kgosi had started to really distance himself from Masego, choosing instead to go out with the boys most of the time. They would spend most of their allowance money on alcohol, clothes and anything that would make them more popular. There were also rumors going around on campus that Kgosi was cheating on Masego-something that really sank her heart. She would conjure up enough strength to ask him if this was true and he would deny it-something she was hoping he would do. But a girl as smart as Masego should know better, right?! This was also around the same time that Kgosi started selling weed to supplement his lifestyle, although he didn't smoke it.

As Kgosi became more popular, varsity became more of showing off your materialism and not your intellectualism. He was gaining more followers on social media and had even become known as the ambassador of *colorism*, always pitting girls against each other online based off of their skin-tone-the light skinned versus dark-skinned dynamic—which one would make a better girlfriend, or rather, a better girlfriend to be seen with. Masego was witnessing all of this happening and she felt as if she was losing Kgosi and could not do anything about it. As girls would throw themselves at him, he would entertain them, sometimes in the worst way and she would still forgive him knowing very well what he was doing. Apparently, the heart wants what it wants so can you blame her?

One day, Kgosi decided to go into the cocaine business. Most people know that cocaine is much more expensive than weed and therefore, could be a lucrative business, he thought to himself. He however made the mistake of trying it one time when he and the boys were going to the newly opened pub in Riverwalk[9]. His addiction came from using it once. When Masego found out, she asked him to quit or she would end their relationship. He promised to quit but relapsed a week later but somehow kept his composure and thus Masego never found out about his relapse.

One night when Kgosi and Masego were meeting in her room for movie night, something that was kind of a ritual at this point, while he was in the bathroom, a text came in on his phone and out of curiosity she grabbed his phone and read the text. It read: "*Let's link up tomorrow night bro, there's a house party in Block 8*[10] *and there's gonna be coke. We'll take it to the head*" and it was from one of his boys. Her heart shattered and she was so astonished that she couldn't gather enough strength to ask him about the text. Perhaps it was a wrong number or a text sent to him by mistake. The next morning, after class, she finally had the courage to ask him about the text. He tried to deny it but she could see right through him. She ended their relationship right then and there. He didn't see it as a loss but saw it as an opportunity to do more of all the things he couldn't do because he was in a relationship. He felt free now.

Best friends and lovers had now turned into strangers. A week later, Kgosi got caught by a security guard on campus with cocaine and was reported to the school management. This called for an immediate expulsion but he begged management not to report him to the police as he would not dare repeat what he did again-promising also to check himself into rehab, which he never did. His expulsion also meant that he was kicked out of campus with immediate effect and that DTEF would make his sponsorship null and void. He tried to reach out to his "boys" but none of them wanted to be associated with him at all. Some friends *they* are. Because he never told his mother about his expulsion, he couldn't go back home either. So he stayed in Gabs, roaming the streets looking for small odd jobs that would at least pay him enough to get him through the night as well as to feed his coke craving. See, coke is a relatively expensive drug but his *plug* gave him a discount because of his loyalty.

Telling himself that he didn't need school anyway, he went around the city looking for any job he could do and managed to find some which were never long-term but they enabled him to find a small one-roomed house to rent in Tlokweng[11]. He then found a job doing garden work close to where he was renting. A couple of months later, the owners of the house where he would labor every morning had to move because they bought a house in a better neighborhood. Kgosi didn't let his landlady know as he thought he'd find another *piece job* soon enough but that wasn't the case. After failing to pay his rent for the second month in a row, his landlady, being the understanding person that she was, decided to give him one more month to come up with the rent he owed. He even thought about going back to Oodi at one point but the disappointment and hurt he would bring unto his mother made him think twice-let alone the fact that he was now a junkie as well.

As the end of the last month his landlady had given him was approaching, things were looking bleak for Kgosi. He tried to contact one of his boys from varsity again but instead of the phone just ringing, it wasn't going through at all, suggesting that his number had been blocked. Getting back into varsity looked more and more like a pipe dream. Where was he going to get the *P22 000* per semester that was needed for his course? If he was to turn his life around, where was he going to get the amount needed to check himself into rehab? How was he going to maneuver through all this without his people back at home finding out? Unable to come up with any logical answer to any of these questions, suicidal thoughts came to his mind-the easiest thing to do. This was the solution that would solve all his problems. Now the only thing left would be to figure out how he was going to do it. Using a rope came to his mind and he contacted his landlady asking for a rope. He told her that he wanted to use it to make a leash for a stray puppy he had found in the yard. And so, she just happened to have some rope in her toolshed. He went to her place to collect it and she saw this as an opportunity to remind him that three months' worth of rent was due in a few days. He concurred and rushed back home as he didn't want to waste any more time.

• • ❧ • •

FIVE MINUTES BEFORE he wrapped the noose around his neck, he received a text from his ex-girlfriend whom he still loved very much-the love of his life. She wanted to meet up and talk-A glimpse of hope as he rushed to put his shoes on, slam the door behind him and venture on this exciting and promising quest, forgetting even, to lock the door. The combi[12] he was on was moving too slowly for his liking and to him it felt like the driver was conspiring against him getting his lady back; Mr. Driver, the villain.

As soon as the combi reached his stop, he gave the driver his fare and bolted towards the park that was the agreed destination. He found Masego on one of the benches patiently waiting, on her phone, looking as beautiful as he remembered her to be. Pausing for a few seconds, he had to soak it all in and a feeling of joy almost overwhelmed him. Masego looked up as if she could sense his presence without him having to say or do anything to let her know he was there. They greeted each other with a warm and lengthy hug. Kgosi told her all about the plan to end his own life because he felt he had lost everything that was dear to him, including his sense of who he was. He told her how earlier that day, a few minutes before he decided to go through with his plan, he got her text and that's what *saved* him. Masego, being the great listener that she was, sat there and allowed him to pour out his feelings to his satisfaction.

Hearing all this brought much sadness to her heart, even to the point that she shed a tear as a result. When it was her turn to talk, she told him how much he had hurt her with his shenanigans, how *she* almost lost herself because of it, how it took her a while to come to terms with losing her best friend and lover. She told him that she forgives him but they cannot get back together because it's going to be a while before she can trust anyone with her heart again. However, she did tell him that she missed her *bestie*[13] in her life and was willing to give him another chance as exactly that for the time being and who knows what the future holds-that the universe might plot something more.

Kgosi understood the magnitude of his actions and was thus willing to deal with the consequences. He told her that whatever she had in mind was enough for him as long as she was on his side again, promising her that he would work on getting his act together, if not for himself then all for her. Contemplating the events that took place from when he left Oodi till now, he realized how not everyone is as lucky as he was to get a second chance at life-something that propelled him further in his actions to better himself. This was the beginning of how Kgosi intended to get his lady and life back.

After the heartfelt conversation between the two, they decided to walk to the bus rank together instead of taking a combi. It was a lengthy distance but not impossible. Oblivious to the setting sun, they traveled and at one point, Masego felt a tingle of fright come over her body as though someone was following them but Kgosi quickly dismissed it as a usual sunset breeze. There was already less movement of people as it was getting darker and although Masego advised against it, the charmingly convincing lad convinced her that taking a shortcut was the best option for them to get to the bus rank quicker. As they did so, a muscular individual wearing a balaclava came out of nowhere to the two former lovebirds' surprise. Everything happened so suddenly that once Masego conjured up the strength to scream for help, she found herself staring at a seemingly lifeless body that lay in a trench surrounded by blood with a note beside the body. The distraught lass overwhelmed by shock picked up the note and it read, "*You didn't think you could hustle me and get away with it, did you, my boy*?!" A jogger found Masego sitting next to the body, head lying on her chest unable to talk and called an ambulance.

• • ❧ • •

1. A Setswana name meaning chief/king.
2. A village in the Kgatleng District of Botswana. It is located 20 km north-east of Gaborone (Botswana's capital city).
3. A Setswana name meaning an abundance of luck.
4. A senior secondary school located at Gaborone in the South Central region of Botswana.
5. The second largest city in Botswana located in eastern Botswana, about 400 KMs north-northeast from the capital, Gaborone.
6. Botswana's capital city.
7. An informal, shortened word for Gaborone used by the locals.
8. An annual entertainment event hosted by the student representative councils of tertiary schools to welcome first years to their experience of varsity.
9. The first shopping mall in Gaborone located along the road that leads to the Tlokweng border.
10. A suburb located in the South-East District of Botswana

within Gaborone.

11. A village located directly adjacent to Gaborone in the South-east District and is on the road to the border with South Africa, the border post being just 15km to the east.
12. A term used by the locals referring to public transport vehicles that carry up to 15 passengers.
13. An informal word that refers to a best friend.

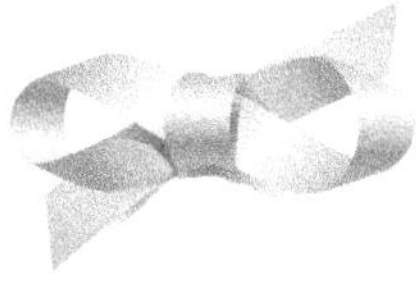

CHAPTER 3 – AFRO-FUTURISM

So much greatness that once permeated the motherland has been forgotten overtime. This does not mean the greatness is non-existent. Some of the elements were so ahead of their time that they can still be utilized to this day to visualize a technologically-advanced future society.

Transition

It is the year 2049 and humans exist in a fully-fledged technological society. Mutulu Bengaota is a Kenyan polymath born in 1980 who, since 2005, has been involved in bringing, as well as encouraging, a more technological mindset and approach of solving, first, national issues or problems, and then continental ones thereafter. He was one of the few people from his country and the continent of Africa to suggest a better approach to dealing with the education of the youth by calling schools out to take on a teaching approach that promotes *how* to think rather than *what* to think, and thus allow them an opportunity to be innovative in whatever field they may choose. Some of his peers, in hindsight, have come to refer to him as someone *way* ahead of his time.

There were always debates amongst scholars about whether or not the *Extremely Low Frequency* (ELF) waves emitted from the screens of devices such as, television monitors and more especially personal computers were radioactive and could ultimately lead to causing some form of cancer within the human body. The overall consensus reached in the year 2000, between various top medical doctors and scientists across the earth was that the effects these waves had on the body were negligible—which may/may not have been the case at that point in time due to perhaps a lack of more advanced tools of experiment. Oh, how the devil would be proud of such advocacy!

Mutulu grew up in a family of three kids. He is the youngest with two older sisters both in the *FinTech* sector. As a matter of fact, they were in the financial sector initially, and then got introduced to the tech side of it through their little brother's research. Their father is an engineer and inventor in his own right, well known in the town of *Thika*[1], where he raised his children. Their mom was a teacher at a nearby school, now retired. So from a young age, all the three kids had education, learning and being solution-driven, with sincerity and a tincture of modesty as their foundation. It only makes sense that Mutulu grew up to be as great as he has been deemed to be.

At the age of 15, Mutulu built his first personal computer (PC) from scratch, using parts he bought from a local spare-part shop and some scraps from the dumping site. He had researched on the theoretical process of building such devices from scratch and the tools he'd need, and then saved up some of the money he received as payment from working with his father at his repairs shop on the weekend. He taught himself how to code using *COBOL*, *PHP*, *JavaScript*, *HTML* and *CSS*, and continued to learn in alignment with whatever is relevant at the time. This was the routine every day after school and somehow he managed. School became more interesting to him in the sense that, he noticed there was a need for tech and all the things he was learning in his spare time, but for some reason, most of those lessons were either not included within the curriculum or their importance not being emphasized enough.

Studying all these concepts by himself gave him an advantage over other students in his class when he enrolled in an *Information Communication Technology* (ICT) course at *Thika Technical Training Institute* (Thika TTI). Graduating top of his class, Thika TTI paid for his ticket and accommodation to a Science and Technology conference to be held in Kigali, Rwanda later in that year. Throughout his course, he had been utilizing his parents' garage to teach some of the youth in his hometown what he had taught himself. The space wasn't huge and those who came to learn had to take turns. He insisted on doing it for free, which was the initial agreement but after a few lessons, those he was teaching suggested they donate a small amount to him as a token of appreciation. He'd assist his dad on Fridays and Saturdays and reserve Sundays for his "students".

Completing his Thika TTI course didn't mean the end of school/ learning for Mutulu. There were now online short courses he could partake in to supplement his research. He could finally afford his first *proper* pc, looked for a small secure warehouse near his home that he could use for his students, and as time went on, invested in a few desktop computers as part of his practical lessons. Whilst still teaching himself how to code, one of the things he realized was that there was a gap that existed in the tech space regarding various organizations of business and otherwise. Mutulu went to his sisters for advice on how to leverage this and leverage it, he did. Building sample websites, he went to different organizations to pitch to them this idea about how this is where technology was headed, and what they needed to market themselves to not only retain current clients but gain new ones as well. He even attempted to get some of them to invest in his "crazy" ideas he had come up with after his return *voyage* from the conference in Kigali. Investment was a bit of a far reach and he *sort of* knew it, so rejection there came as no surprise. Even though most organizations declined his marketing pitch, some took heed and short-term agreements with minor payments were made as a means of *testing the waters*.

In 2010, Mutulu started a Research and Development (R&D) company called *BengaCorp*, focusing on researching current and future technologies that could assist in solving everyday problems such as grocery shopping, reading someone's energy and identifying what issue they may be having or what mood they may be in and bring up suggestions on how to best deal with *grey* energy moods like depression, etcetera. BengaCorp was the first company of its kind in Kenya that, not only hired varsity graduates but non-graduates as well, some from the *famous* garage. Anyone with a passion for tech and solving problems by thinking innovatively was an automatic winner for Mutu.

Being pen-pals with and a mentor to Laone for over a decade, an aspiring *technopreneur*, Mutu, got this crazy idea, in 2020, to partner up with Laone and open up a small R&D company in Botswana that learns from BengaCorp but is its own entity focusing on providing solutions unique to Botswana. All the disruption that was now taking place because of the advancement of technology came as no surprise to Mutu. He had researched on it, saw it coming and was prospering off of his preparations. Laone was heading up the R&D company in Botswana and received some wise words from her mentor regarding having patience, perseverance and resilience when it comes to the tech space on the continent in general.

• • ❧ • •

2035 WAS A ROUGH YEAR for Mutu. He got diagnosed with stage 2 *Ewing Sarcoma*[2], which was rare, especially at his age. It wasn't hereditary. After inquiring as to his daily routine, his doctors asserted that the ELF waves from all the computer screens, electronic monitors and other technologies devices he was surrounded by on the daily over a period of time caused the cancer. Chemotherapy worked but the cancer came back after eight years, spreading even quicker. Mutu refused to undergo chemo this time because of its side effects. Doctors told him he had a good shot at beating it once more and if he didn't undergo chemo, he'd not survive for too long. Still, he turned it down and his doctors told him the best they could do was keep him alive for at most six years. They also suggested that Mutu could transfer his consciousness into a *Synthetic*[3] but he turned down the offer letting them know that he wanted to *retain his humanness*—that his whole vision wasn't to become a machine but rather to put machines in a position of external assistance to human beings so *trans-humanism* was out of the picture for him.

Although Mutu had accepted his fate, he still had faith that somehow a more fitting and less painful solution would present itself. And so, it did. In those six years, his cells started mutating as if they were responding to his *foolish* zeal for healing. His body began healing itself as if now adapting to the external technological environment. Neither him nor his doctors could believe it and began to study his cells. Towards the end of 2048, his cancer was gone. Asking him what he would do different going forward, he told his doctors that he realized *the greatest evolution occurs from within* and in 2049, would refocus his company with this approach in mind.

1. An industrial town and major commerce hub in Kiambu County, Kenya.
2. A type of cancer that may be a bone sarcoma or soft-tissue sarcoma.
3. A non-human entity regarded by law as having the status of a person.

Out of the Matrix

Sebaga is prepping for her final exam before graduation. Her lecturer, Mrs. Kigali, is based in Rwanda and is about to connect to her via the internet for her final practical. For this demonstration, she'll be using her *virtual reality* glasses to bring the resources she needs to where she is. Mrs. K is a qualified cryptologist with quite some experience to her name. It is time and the call comes in. Sebaga's lecturer is now connected live to her through her computer monitor. Sebaga goes all out and demonstrates her understanding of *cryptocurrencies*, the ins and outs of *blockchain* and how to go about mining *CosmoCoin* effectively and efficiently. So far, Mrs. K seems greatly impressed as she writes her analyses in her notepad. Graduation for Sebaga means that she'll now have the proper skills to join the other countless cryptocurrency miners all around the African continent. Her lecturer is delighted to tell her that she's passed her practical with a 97%, congratulates her and lets her know that she'll receive a soft copy of her certificate of completion in two days or the hardcopy in two weeks. The new graduate is unable to conceal her joy as she bids farewell to Mrs. K. The first person she calls is her bestie, Maipelo. A celebration is brewing.

CosmoCoin is a digital/crypto currency coin, backed by an abundant resource on the continent called *Ambronium*[*], that leaders of various African nations came up with after financial advice from within their nations that the traditional banking system would fall in a few years. They engaged in talks with their citizens and found that there were few individuals who were self-taught in the field and therefore called upon these individuals to spearhead campaigns of teaching what they knew to the rest of their people. After deliberations and discussions, decisions were also made that one currency would suffice for the entire continent for day-to-day transactions within and across nations.

It is the year 2073 EA (Evolutionary Age) and in the past three decades the African continent has made huge strides in spiritual, psychological, physiological and financial advancements to name a few. The name of the continent has also been altered to reflect its current state. *Afura Faso* is a name that has been agreed upon by appointed leaders, meaning *Land of Abundance, Prosperity and Wealth*. These leaders formed and are members of the *Afura Faso Council of Leaders* (AFCL). They are leaders of different nations on the continent and are elected by the people based off of both left brain and right brain hemispheric balance and functioning, thereby leading by example.

Afurabés[*] in every nation are a united community of extremely intelligent and highly intuitive individuals with a deeply cultivated and highly accurate level of discernment. With an average continental literacy rate of 98%, every nation is also a society of creative, highly spiritual, compassionate and highly innovative individuals that have activated most of their DNA due to the high quality of education they receive nationally as well as continentally. This education stems from and emphasizes *universal* law. Due to this, low-level and high-level crimes are virtually non-existent. Every citizen of every nation is responsible for his/her own thoughts and actions and therefore simply knows better. From a young age, they undergo a year of home-schooling to equip them with the basic tools they need to trigger both left brain and right brain activity, as well as basic principles and their significance, that permeate the entire continental society such as oneness. These citizens, thus grow up with the fundamental and foundational ability to operate directly from the heart through their actions.

For higher learning, there are quite a number of universities across the continent that offer courses such as *Philosophy*, *Astrological Metaphysics, Psychology*, *Masonry*, *Mythology*, *Arts*, *Quantum Mathematics* (which includes *Sacred Geometry* and *Gematria*), *Cryptocurrency,* that also covers setting up a basic blockchain network moving up to a more advanced network and *Quantum Science* covering, sound therapy, communication through sound and light with seeds and plants to increase yields, as well as other sciences dealing with using sound and light to form and deform matter at the sub-atomic level.

Regardless of individuals being from different Afura Faso nations, there is one language that most, if not all, recognize—the language of *symbols*. This language is taught under Mythology for individuals who opt for higher learning. Depending on the culture, tradition and location of each nation, most Afurabés build their houses in hexagonal shapes, decorated with ancient symbols in honor of ancient civilizations and to signify oneness of the people and their understanding of being a bridge between the past and the future. They make a living through mostly what they are passionate about. There are musicians, painters, philosophical economists, psychological cryptologists, holistic healers, physiological masons, hydro-mythologists, aura-cleansers, poetic eschatologists, and etcetera.

The universities offer their courses on-campus and through virtual classrooms. The choice depends on the prospective student. Every nation has at least four of such universities teaching similar courses that differ according to the culture of the nation. Each of these universities, however, have six levels students have to go through before embarking on the quest to find a seventh and final level. Six of the lower levels are pre-requisites for the main courses (students have to choose at least two as the main). Main courses begin with the seventh level. Completion of the seventh level is simultaneous with completion of a student's courses, paving the way for graduation and being regarded as practically astute in the fields they've been studying for.

The first level is called the *Red Self*, dealing with grounding the individual. Secondly, the *Orange Self*, dealing with an individual's interactions with the people around them. Thirdly is the *Yellow Self* that deals with personal willpower and self-esteem. The fourth level is the *Green Self*, which is quite a challenge for a lot of people. It deals with love, internal balance and compassion for others. Communication and self-expression comes next under the *Purple Self* followed by the *Indigo Self*, dealing with telepathy, travelling to parallel worlds, as well as travelling to different places without one's physical body and being fully aware of it, amongst other things. Each level takes about six months to complete.

The seventh level is the *Violet Self* and has no set time frame. It involves lessons on how to open and close gateways to other dimensions, create whole new worlds and use time *whenever* necessary to create a database across dimensions. Classrooms for this level are built as mud huts for a specific reason and are hidden to students of the lower three levels. This reason is unraveled by the student once they find the classrooms and partake in the classes. Violet Self classrooms remain partly hidden to the fourth, fifth and sixth levels and are only fully visible to the frequency of love. One extremely important module that is studied together with lessons in these levels is *Mental Health & Mind Magic*. It is here where students learn how to spot trauma in them first, then others through human behavior and confront it in order to deal with it by solving or *dissolving* it. This is so as it is trauma that mostly leads to blockages in human evolution.

An advanced form of Mind Magic is taught at the Violet Self level where students learn how to consciously commit to memory and recollection of past memories regardless of the time-frame with minimum effort. Another lesson is on ways of expanding their mental capacity and using their imagination together with intuition and intellect to solve relatively small and relatively large problems/issues. It is also here that more advanced practical lessons on telepathy and teleportation with and without the physical body are held.

• • ❧ • •

BEGINNING OF 2053, the AFCL has come up with a number of *clean* technological strategies and policies to assist their people without bringing harm up to the environment. Citizens savvy in technology, mathematics, engineering and the like were engaged to build technologies that harness solar energy, providing electricity to each and every individual in need of it, and store excess solar energy to induce rain during drier months for hydro-electric power plants. Also part of the mandate was to build structures that would be able to harness the moon's energy as part of healing mechanisms for individuals in hospitals. These are just *some* of the things that the AFCL has implemented and have nearly-perfected with on-going improvements.

One of the other things that the AFCL has put into place is the ability for citizens all across the continent to utilize CosmoCoin in every nation for any type of transactions. This has enabled the currency to stay longer and rotate within the continent. Because of this, citizens are able to get 70% university sponsorship anywhere within the continent. They are also able to get funding from within their own nations for their start-ups if they assist with mining CosmoCoin thus adding more value back into the economy. AFCL has also secured trade agreements with the rest of the world using CosmoCoin. Every nation boasts at least three majorly advanced research and development facilities focusing on new and emerging technologies that may assist in improving its citizens' quality of life and standard of living, partly funded by the council and partly funded by citizens that volunteer to do so.

Sebaga is from Botswana and she's one of the miners of CosmoCoin. She now has a start-up company developing devices that scan the body's organs in three dimensions and full color for any ailments, and a supplementary app to make it easier for one to diagnose oneself from the comfort of their own home. It uses green technology and does relatively no harm to the human body. Her start-up is one of those that received funding from the council. Mrs. K is now next in line for a seat at the AFCL.

During the Evolutionary Age that started in the year 2020, the veil is being lifted and Afura Faso is not as dark as it once was deemed. Or rather, it should be said that out of the darkness comes light—either way, Afurabés are coming out of the matrix and a vast amount of possibilities and opportunities lie within their reach. The ball is really in their court.

*Afura Faso is a fictional name.

*Ambronium is a fictional name.

*Afurabé refers to any citizen of the Afura Faso continent. Afurabés is the plural.

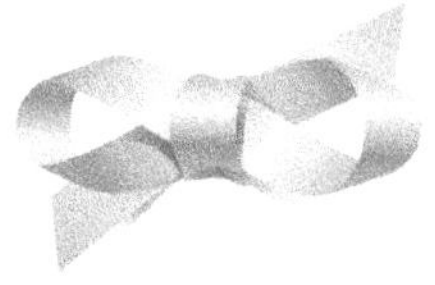

CHAPTER 4 – AFRO-MYTHOS, ADVENTURE AND FANTASY

If darkness harbors potential energy, then potential energy is neither your friend nor your enemy. The stars reiterate the same narrative by being naturally magnificent. I shall embrace the darkness. It is where I'll make the greatest discoveries about myself and take heed of the messages the stars are trying to communicate.

Encounters with the Yellow Goddess

During the night of the full moon, the dogs howl as if to send their prayers to the big silver ball in the sky. Emotions have been high these past few days and it appears that on days like these, many people lose control of their emotions unbeknownst to them as to why it is so.

Such is an observation Lone has been making for quite a while as a self-proclaimed student of nature. Earlier in the day, she had sent a resignation email to her boss and all she can attribute her *irrational* decision to is her feeling of unhappiness from the working environment—feeling as though the company's vision was no longer the same as when she arrived there. The excitement of her being part of a tech startup and being there from inception to where it had gotten had died down—partly due to the now financial turmoil the company was experiencing. She quit with no plan B, C or D but at least she had a few bucks in her savings account. Mama had taught her well. Mama also understood her reasons for quitting and stood by her.

A year later, Lone had depleted her funds and was now relying on her mom for a lot of things. The little she was getting from hustles wasn't enough let alone consistent enough for her to contribute to the household. She had sent applications to multiple tech companies over the period but to no avail. Luckily her mom was there for all the support she needed, especially mentally and emotionally but she could see how straining it was becoming on her mom. Her journal made sure her mind wasn't idle enough to be the devil's playground. The foolish heroine was starting to wonder if she had made the right decision by leaving her *dream-job,* starting to feel less and less in control of this movie she called her life.

Another year passed and on the two year anniversary of that now rueful day, Lone was now at a very low point in her life. Again, that night happened to fall on a full moon. Before heading to bed, she gazed at the beauty of the big silver ball in the sky, reflecting on what had become of her life. Letting out a deep sigh, she bid her mother a goodnight and retreated to her room. She usually had trouble sleeping but on this particular night, as soon as she laid her head on her *Black Panther* pillow, she dozed off.

That night, she had a very vivid dream that she was surprisingly aware of while it was taking place. Finding herself in a bright yellow building made of sun-flower and hieroglyph stained glass, what impressed her even more was how as she approached the walls and tried to touch them, they moved even further away from her, coming to the conclusion that the building wasn't confined to one space. It went on and on into the far distance.

While still admiring the building's architecture, a distorted ball of light, slightly a darker shade of yellow approached Lone. Astonished at the site, she moved back but immediately, a familiar voice reassured her of her safety and well-being. As the ball of light got closer to her, it began to form into a familiar site to go with the voice she had heard. That familiar site was her mother but she was surrounded by a glowing bright yellow field of light. Lone began dialog and asked if what she was seeing was in actuality her mom. The *being* told her that it wasn't but had to take a form that Lone knew well and trusted. "What are you and what are we doing here?" asked Lone. The being took a bit of time and responded, "I have quite a few names. You may refer to me as you wish. The important thing is that you know that I'm part of the *Priestesshood of Intui*.

"Your people on Earth have called me by various names. And they have elevated me to the level of Goddess. Our job as the Priestesshood is to assist residents of the Earth with paths that lead to the answers they may have questions to—but only *if* they ask. If they do not, then we cannot be much of service, even if we feel a strong urge to!" Lone took a deep breath as if to digest all that had just been said. "That is interesting. Why are you telling me this?" asked Lone. "My child, I have noticed that you're going through a tough phase in your life currently and all I want to do is to assure you that you made the right choice by leaving that toxic environment two years ago. It wasn't going to end well and I need you to stop beating yourself up about it.

"The feeling you got before you put together that resignation email was me encouraging you to think about yourself and get rid of things that may be of detriment to your well-being. You have many gifts and talents. You should explore them all. Especially that of writing!" said the being. Lone let out a tear and a sigh, "I knew I had to trust the feeling but I didn't know why. So glad I do now though. Now I see why my people worship you!" exclaimed Lone. "To some extent, I do too but that is not my intention. I do not want you to worship me. Oh no. What I do want is for you to acknowledge my presence and celebrate it by celebrating yourself—celebrating all your parts and leaving out nothing. Do it even when it feels confusing. Do it when you get an urge to and do it well. In that way, you will be honoring the both of us and that is all that I want-Especially for you, my child!" the being responded.

Immediately after the dialog, Lone woke up, looked at the time on her phone, *3:33am*, recorded the dream in her journal, then went back to sleep. Upon her waking, she bolted into her mom's room to share the dream with her only to find the room vacant. Luckily, she heard a sweeping sound outside the house—a sound that speedily exposed her mom's whereabouts. Upon being in Mama Gloria's presence, she narrated her dream experience but her mom took it in with a grain of salt—something Lone already expected. Before she could write her mom off entirely, Mama Gloria seized her daughter's hand before she had the opportunity to leave and led her to a shade by one of the mango trees in her garden. They sat down on a rock that seemed to have been carved for this very purpose before the garden existed. Lone's mom meticulously explained how she used to get similar dreams when she was younger with the difference being that hers would include strangers that she would later meet after they made an appearance in her dreams. "Ah, mama! How come you've never told me about any of this?" asked Lone. "My child, I would dream of very strange things that even now, I cannot articulate to you. My mother also kept on encouraging me to dismiss whatever it is that I thought I saw in the dreams, probably out of fear for her life and especially mine. You know we live in an extremely superstitious society. I took heed of her sentiments. So after a while, the dreams just stopped," said Mama Gloria. "I'm so sorry to hear that, mama." Lone's mom responded, "Oh, don't worry too much about me, ngwanaka. My time is almost up. I've lived my life. It's time to live yours. You're a special child. I've known that from the day you were born. Even your father knew it. It's sad he had to leave us before he could witness your blooming. What I need you to do is to live your life to the best of your ability, authentically. Like the message in your dream, don't ever feel like you need to hide any parts of yourself to impress anyone! And remember, I'm with you always, my child. My support for whatever path you feel is calling you is a given. Ke a go rata. I love you!" "Wow, this was unexpected. Thank you Mama. For this chat and for incessantly being my rock. Your words have not fallen on deaf ears. I love you too."

The two's session adjourned with a hug as Mama Gloria got up to return to her garden obligations. Lone went back into the house, back into her room, opened her journal and put her dream into a story that she submitted for a competition at an online publishing platform. Six weeks later, the platform responded letting her know she had won the competition. She was ecstatic and couldn't wait to share the news with her mom. The prize money also helped—a lot!

Lone continued to churn out story after story daily but did not let the stories out to the public due to a bit of self-doubt that kept on creeping in. Three weeks after the competition she had won, she received an email from a publishing company stating that they read her winning story and were inquiring if she'd be interested in a paying three year book publishing deal. Overwhelmed, Lone had an epiphany that this was what the turbulent two year phase was paving a way for and that maybe, just maybe her journal actually had gems.

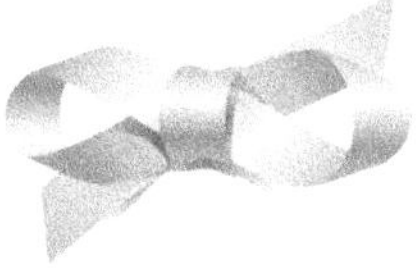

Of Flying Things

There once lived a beautiful girl on the outskirts of a village that took much pride in its culture and tradition stemming back tens of thousands of years. Her name was Khumo and she lived with her great grandmother next to a river regarded sacred by the elders in that area. The two lived a simple life, utilizing solar energy for electricity in their thatch roof bungalow although they didn't need it much. Most of the dwellings in the village followed the same simple but effective structure. The two had everything they needed and this was largely due to the supportive community in which they lived. Khumo's great grandma, Mary was a medicine woman and oracle and this added very much to her celebrated status in their community. Besides that, most people generally gave respect and reverence to the elderly. The older one was the more life experience they had and the wiser they were believed to be; which in most cases, they were. Mary raised Khumo from the age of three and home-schooled her. She witnessed the timid little girl she adored oh so very much blossom into an exuberant and especially curious adolescent with the help of her community.

On some nights, an eager member of the community would whip up a scrumptious meal and dish up for the two with the intention of going over to Gogo Mary's for a folktale or three. Mary would facetiously roll her eyes at the sight of a familiar individual rushing towards her house with a container filled to the brim in their hands as she heartily prepared for their arrival. Khumo would set up a fire near the river and the tales would flow out of the highly retentive and articulate storyteller. In a short while, they would be joined by some of the children for an unparalleled outdoor experience—a habit that had become a norm at this point.

• • ❧ • •

KHUMO'S PARENTS, *Kabelo* and *Queen* met their untimely passing when she was only three years. A drunk driver ran a red light one rainy night in the city and that was it. The young couple, was returning home following a romantic night out to celebrate their fourth anniversary and were still alive, although barely when the medics arrived on the scene and rushed to the nearest hospital. In the wreckage also lay the male driver who looked barely thirty. The metal from his car had sandwiched him in such a way that his last words were a plea to the medics not to attempt to move anything as he felt the pain was already excruciating. A few moments after he uttered those words, he succumbed to his injuries.

The two survivors turned warriors were in the intensive care unit (I.C.U) for three weeks and fought for their lives with the assistance of the medical team on duty on those gloomy nights. By their side day in and day out were the hopeful but realistic Mary and the innocently oblivious young Khumo. A weak pulse demonstrated by the electrocardiogram (ECG) machine became the norm, and on one tragic Sunday night, the exhausted but resilient medical team hastened into the comatose couple's room after a young interning nurse doing her rounds heard a perturbing sound from the ECG machine. An entire hour went by as the team utilized the defibrillator the best they could in an attempt to get Kabelo's pulse back but to no avail. It's almost as if though, Queen, in her unconscious state, could feel this tragedy as it occurred and opted not to leave her husband's side no matter where he went.

• • ❧ • •

THE SACRED-NESS OF the river the two lived next to would be underscored by its beauty at night. It would glisten with many colors, some from what we know as a rainbow, some so exotic, even describing them was a mammoth of a task. One would think that members of the community would come rushing to view this spectacle as it happened but Mary would, to her despair later come to discover that very few people had the eyesight for it. Not even the elders were privy to it except one or two and they knew the reasons for this long before Mary did.

Mary would sit outside for a lengthy period of time on these nights, especially under a clear sky, and talk to the water as if it were alive. A heated dialog seemed to validate this *far-fetched* notion. One of the things she'd talk to the body of water about was her dreams. Out of curiosity, Khumo, from a very young age of five would ask her aging, but still quite energetic great grandma why she shared her dreams with the river and she'd explain to her that the river assisted her greatly with interpreting her dreams. These weren't just dreams that were personal to her but those that related to the community at large. Matter of fact, their village had seen many seasons of peace courtesy of such dreams.

• • ❧ • •

ONE OF THE TRADITIONS still practiced in the village was that of asking for rain—a ritual that all members of the community partook in. In the summer months, the village Chief and elders would gather their people by the sacred river, on the first Saturday of the first summer month before the sun rises. There'd be chants, mantras and dances aimed at the sky corresponding to the beat of the drums, followed by a collective trance. This trance would release a ball of energy engulfing the Chief, serving as protection as he/she traveled into the river to deliver his/her people's requests, till totally submerged and would only come out as the first rays of the blistering, desert-like sun hit the surface of the river. A vortex-like opening would show itself as the Chief entered and this was regarded as a welcoming gesture—one that would cause further excitement for the rest of the people and an increased loudness of chants and mantras.

The Chief's emergence from the depths of the waters was greeted by ululations from the people and seen as a sign that their requests were heard and it would be a very productive and abundant summer in terms of rainfall leading to an abundance of harvest. Failure of the Chief's emergence meant the opposite and ultimately, the death of the Chief. They would have been *swallowed by the waters*. There were such rituals and then there was initiation which was rather more personal than collective, albeit the community *did* come together to celebrate the completion of the initiation ceremony on a specific agreed date.

• • ❧ • •

KHUMO WAS A DREAMER too; Quite a graphic one to say the least. She would dream of familiar and unfamiliar individuals both living and non-living, with wings and they would be differentiated by the color surrounding their bodies. Some of these individuals would be the color *only* without a body. There'd be people riding white-colored horses that had wings on them, rainbow-colored dragons that would offer her rides into nothingness and she'd accept willingly, rainbow-colored serpents with wings slithering back and forth as if to compel her to follow them somewhere, and birds both smaller and larger than any she'd seen. In one of her recurring dreams, she was sitting out in nature, surrounded by different species of trees that were as tall as her eyes could see with large green canopies of leaves. While there, she saw a relatively tiny dark brownish bird with a rust-brown tail that landed next to where she was sitting. As the dream recurred over a few nights, the number of birds of the same species would increase. The birds would be there beside her in silence, and then let out one or two chirps, as if to gain her attention before resorting back to silence again. While there, the birds would also flap their wings continuously and in that moment, she'd feel it in her core that this bird was her soul communicating with her, bringing her a deep sense of peace within the dream and as she woke up.

All these entities would attempt to communicate with her in these dreams either through speech, symbols or telepathically but she didn't know what it all meant. What was the purpose of all the dreams? How did they impact her life? How were they *going to* impact her life, if at all? These were some of the questions she would ask her captivated great grandma as these dreams were being relayed to her. Mary was older than Khumo when she started having similar dreams and they weren't as vivid. The dreams also weren't coming through as vigorous as they were for Khumo. Of course, Mary explained them as best she could in a manner someone as young as her obviously gifted great granddaughter could comprehend. During those moments, she knew that Khumo would highly likely soon enough dream of the beginning of her initiation process to take over her great grandma's work in the community. As custom, the initiate dreamt of the person, usually an elder, to initiate them into *whatever* gift they were born with. That's the only time this type of ritual of initiation was carried out and carried out by village elders.

One day, great grandma Mary had a house call. A son had rushed to her from the other side of the village following his mother's sudden illness. He arrived at Mary's house hysterical and she had to calm him down with some chamomile tea so he could state the purpose of his visit and his laments. She however could also see from the boy's one shoe, panting and trembling body that whatever it was, was serious. Karabo, he said his name was, did his best to tell his story but before he could finish, Mary grabbed her medicine bag, grabbed Karabo's tiny hand, bid the empathic and understanding Khumo farewell and the two went on their way.

An hour later, around three in the afternoon, Khumo decided to let loose and cool off as the unrelenting sun's rays landed on her skin while taking a walk along the riverbank. She decided to go for a swim. She knew the basics, thanks to Mary. The river received her well as the ripples and the waves accompanied her to the deeper parts of it. She swam and swam, disregarding the advance she had made away from where she started. After a short while, she found herself at the deepest part of the river with no one in sight but remained calm overestimating her swimming abilities. While there, pondering on her dreams, her life in general and whether Karabo's mom would recover, something suddenly drew her into the water.

Khumo attempted to scream for help but was discouraged by a sudden doubt that anyone was close enough to heed her distress call and before she knew it, she was deep inside the water, kicking and flapping, kicking and flapping. This struggle was followed by a familiar voice of a woman that told her to relax and let go. As the water was drawing her deeper, Khumo let out a deep exhalation and gave into the waters. Within her surrender, the now tranquil, fearless coming-of-age teen saw a new world filled with flying entities—the same ones she'd dream of. They could hear her albeit there were no utterances coming from her, and she understood them. In that moment, a chill traveled up and down her spine, bringing with it the epiphany that all these entities are no different from her. A moment later, as the young woman was now in a complete state of surrender, offering no resistance at all to the water, letting it do what it pleased with her, she noticed a bird she had seen in one of her dreams. The bird flapped its wings continuously as it usually did and in that moment an overwhelming, inexplicable but somewhat familiar feeling immersed her, annihilating all fear, anxiety and restlessness. Khumo then transformed into the same bird and joined it as it flew towards its kind in the distant and darker waters.

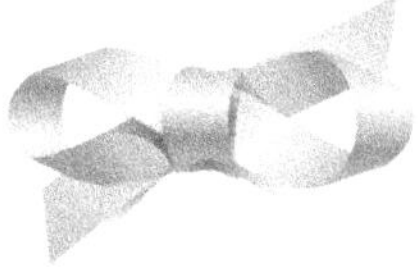

Images of a Nation's Consciousness

As the sun rises, Maipelo (Maps) rushes to the usual meeting place at the top of the mountain. He feels he's a bit late today but he has a good reason. There were chores to be done and it was his turn to do them. Excitement engulfs him albeit this is something he's come to do on the regular—a rendezvous with his closest buddy. Luckily, his buddy hasn't arrived yet and as he approaches the chill spot by the lake, there's a sigh of relief at this realization. A few minutes later, his buddy, nicknamed *Phatsimo* (The Shining One) by him, arrives and the fun begins. The first time they met, there were a lot of questions that Phatsimo had to answer. Luckily, he was willing to do so. "Is this what you truly look like? Are you really a giant?" asked Maps. "Not quite," Phats explained, "This is what we'd look like in physical form on Earth. Truly speaking, we're always one with the elements!"

Phatsimo (Phats) lives on a planet called *Saturnibekum*, in a galaxy mirroring the Earth's Milky Way but in a stellar system. The beings on the planet are smaller planets themselves that, together, make up the whole planet. It is also a planet that changes form depending on the characteristics of the majority of the smaller planets that comprise it. To human beings, he's of a species of tall, navy blue beings that look similar to the ones in the movie *Avatar* but not quite. They ride creatures of the sky, land and water, referred to as *Kgogomodumo* by the ancients of Maps' culture. This is the form he appeared in when he first met Maps. To Phatsimo's surprise, Maps wasn't as astonished as other humans he'd tried to befriend in the past. Out of curiosity, Phats inquired into such composure at the sight of something so unfamiliar to the human eye. Maps then told him that he had once dreamt of such tall beings that emerged from a wormhole and drew them in his journal. "Oh, that was the union making first contact with whoever was receptive to the frequency. I am here representing them. For, we are one!" exclaimed Phats, "The reason for the contact was for recruitment of someone from Earth to join the *Inter-Galactic Union* (I.G.U) as a representative to carry out the same task that I'm currently carrying out, amongst others." He also explained that there were beings/entities of lower vibrations that were trying to usurp the *omniverse*'s energy for their own malicious intents.

Having met at an art exhibition and immediately hitting it off, Maps and Phatsimo have been friends for a while now. For some reason, he hasn't told his mom about this friendship but has hinted it to his little brother, and his little bro is oh so willing to listen to all these adventures his big brother goes on from time to time. They're friends and love these sessions because they learn from each other, although it's kind of hard to believe that someone from Earth would have anything to teach a more advanced being. These two have been meeting every day and on each day, there's something profound that Maps learns from his friend.

One time, Phats relayed to him that every few decades, there's a wave of energy from the *ethers* that washes over the entire omniverse and when it gets to Earth, increases the frequency of the planet and its inhabitants—a *cycle* they were currently in. However, the energy is filtered in various ways for different individuals because they themselves are on different frequencies of operation/existence. Hence why two people can look at the same thing at the same time and give two completely varying descriptions. He then continued to ask Maps if he had ever wondered why he's able to understand what he's saying, even though he's from a different planet in a different galaxy that does not use spoken languages from Earth. Maps having been oblivious to this asked him why and Phats told him that he was actually communicating to him using symbols, translating them into sound using a device that he created specifically for this interaction.

A year later, all the information about what the I.G.U does has been conveyed to Maps. There's also information now that there's a few others of his own species that have shown interest in becoming part of the union. The two friends are chilling at their usual spot, closer now more than ever. Phats tells his friend that he won't always be around but for as long as he can, he'll guide him throughout all the steps needed to be a member of the I.G.U. He explicates that all the work is continuous, and although of great significance to the omniverse, will have to be done from earth without anyone knowing about it unless on a *need-to-know* basis, either till Maps leaves the union or his essence leaves his physical body indefinitely. Maps nods to show his comprehension then asks Phats why he won't tell him his name. Phats jokingly tells him that the name his buddy has chosen for him is his and he claims it with no queries. He also narrates to him that according to his culture, claiming and/or uttering a name denotes that one completely understands and thus embodies the properties of that name. Therefore, he cannot reveal his name to Maps because there are things he still needs to teach him and him revealing his original name, implies that his journey with him has come to an end.

"What will I do when you're gone? I wonder if I'll ever find a friend like you," exclaimed Maps. "Well, when I leave, I won't really be gone. Just close your eyes, say my name and I'll be there," retorted Phats. Phats' statement brings a feeling of warmness over Maps as he feels a bit of the internal sadness fade away. The two friends hug it out and decide to call it a day. What an end to another great day!

Images of a Nation's Consciousness: Part 2

Ten years of friendship has turned into a brotherhood of sorts—the same amount of years that the I.G.U has successfully kept any type of major inter galactic conflict at bay. It's not a length of time to write home about for such a reputable organization but it's still something. The past year has been quite a challenge for Maps and his bro, Kgosi owing to their mom's passing. A ninety year old wise woman that left her children with as many life lessons and gems as she possibly could.

The two brothers had each other and their god aunt who had now opted to stay with them full-time in their mother's house. This humble abode had so many timeless memories that the two siblings weren't ready to let go of just yet—Maps *slightly* more than his little bro. Family woes, pride and egos had gotten the best of some of the extended family. Some also had their own issues to deal with but that didn't vex Maps too much. They weren't really that close with most of them anyway. Maps' biggest support system however, came from his best buddy, Phats. He played a very big role in aiding him out of near chronic depression after his mom's passing and therefore Maps was able to use that to conjure up enough strength to be there for his brother. Financially, the two had enough to keep them going. Their mom had opened a trust fund for them when she first got into teaching and the money definitely came in handy when Kgosi started varsity. He had a passion for business and that was the study he would pursue for three years. Maps would retreat into his mom's basement for the most part of the day when Kgosi is in school and their god aunt is at work. He had turned the basement into a research lab and that was what he was known for—being a tech researcher working for a company that none of the two people he was living with actually knew or had any idea about. A check came in the mail at the end of each month and that was enough to silence any deeper inquiries. Little did they know that the company, the lab and his "profession" was somewhat all a front for something greater. Kgosi would occasionally go down to the *lab* to see his brother in his element but that was as much as he would get.

Maps had a pet lizard and on certain days he would leave the house, take his pet lizard with and travel to the rendezvous point at the mountain top to link up with Phats. At the mountain top, the two would discuss I.G.U tasks to be executed, those that needed completion and those that were forthcoming. On the other side of the mountain resided a body of water Phats described as ancient. He described this body of water as having had memories of all civilizations having existed on the Earth since the beginning of its existence, as well as those before its existence. This body of water had massive intelligence and was thus one of the portals to other worlds. Phats led the way down the mountain towards the body of water as he always does and Maps followed with much sincerity and curiosity. Such an experience never gets old no matter how many times they may have gone through it!

"Still remember how to do it?" Phats asked sarcastically. "Haha. What do you think?!" replied Maps with a minor smirk as he positioned his pet lizard firmly on the ground at a safe distance. He recited a few magical lines and watched as the lizard metamorphosed into a *Kgogomodumo*. Phats didn't need a physical being that resembles his buddy's pet. He already had the mental capacity to think it into existence instantaneously—and so he did. The two friends rode the *beasts* into the water to enter into where the I.G.U headquarters where located. It was a totally different world that was part of that body of water. There was a special fruit that Phats would give Maps to consume that allowed him to respire under water for as long as he had to be submerged within it. The first time he came here, the experience was so mind-bending for him that he gave the credit to hallucinations. Never had he seen such in any of his dreams but immediately asserted to himself that even if it *was* a dream, at least he was taking conscious part in it. "I won't read your mind but I can tell that you have many questions you don't know how to ask," said Phats. "Well, can you blame me? I mean, what *is* this place? Is it real? It's fascinating! I've never seen anything like it before. Ever", retorted Maps. Phats took a deep breath and responded, "It's as real as you want it to be—just like your world. There's not much of a difference.

"Some of my people have asked the same questions since the beginning of our civilization and they have found the answers they seek. Some haven't. For those that haven't, Earth isn't real for them and that doesn't take much away from the task(s) they were born into that world to carry out. I'm sure the same is true for you and your people. Just like the body of water that we came through, there are portals within your own body that when unlocked activate a different/new level of comprehension of the omniverse, why it exists and its residents. This is *that* level for you. So bask in the ambience" Even more astonishing for Maps than his surrounding was the amount of wisdom that his bestie Phats seemed to possess. He digested all of the wisdom as Phats gave him a full tour of the I.G.U headquarters.

Images of a Nation's Consciousness: Part 3

Six inter galactic wars have taken place in the omniverse. Three of which are prehistoric. The last war nearly demolished it. It took place a thousand years before the *current historical era*. At the time, the same wave of energy that was heavily permeating the omniverse when Maipelo and Phatsimo first met was *making its rounds*, causing similar planetary effects to those it was causing on the Earth.

Intelligent beings/entities from across the cosmos had been studying it as was the norm throughout different civilizations in the times they existed. Some of the beings had malicious intents. It was embedded into their nature as they were of a lower vibration. All they knew best was malice and so they caused it. Being very aware of the type of energy that was going around, these entities understood that these bursts of energy came through in cycles and plotted to usurp it in order to utilize it to their advantage. Their level of intelligence made them powerful enough to do exactly that. They attempted to rule over the entire omniverse and had garnered enough resources to make powerful armies that were nigh undefeatable. These armies started off by conquering different planets one by one, then whole galaxies. It wasn't long before more benevolent beings made a pledge to stand up and fight against all the malice—and so they did.

The malefic entities had gotten so powerful and arrogant. This put them in a position to wage a full-on war against those that referred to themselves as the defenders of the omniverse, i.e. the benevolent entities. These defenders of the galaxies lost five of the wars. It was puzzling to them how this could've happened but became obvious the more they focused on their strategies. After careful analysis of these, the *defenders* came to the conclusion that their continuous defeat was due to a lack of proper organization and unity among them. They only came together and united when it was time for war. They were too individualistic in their approach and that had to change. The *Inter-Galactic Union* (I.G.U) was formed as a result. Its main mandate has always been to maintain peace and stability throughout the various galaxies that make up the omniverse.

Phats was one of the defenders and hence became one of the first members of the I.G.U. The I.G.U has sustained inter galactic peace and stability for over three thousand years. However, about twenty years ago, the omniverse was on the brink of a seventh war. This shook things up at the Union and a realization dawned on them that they had become complacent owing to such a long period of inter galactic peace. Maps was now at the helm of the Union utilizing very well, what his friend and mentor had taught him. The stint that the malefic beings had pulled two decades ago, the last kicks of a dying horse, had caused Phats' demise and Maps was adamant on making his buddy's legacy live on through him. This was evident on his work ethic and the strategies he helped implement that curbed the seventh war. Six months before he passed, Phats finally told Maps his true name as a symbol to show that he had taught him everything he could and alluded that he was now as savvy as Phats was with regards to the I.G.U and the omniverse.

• • ❧ • •

BACK AT HOME, KGOSI and Maps had opened a software and hardware production company. Kgosi took care of all the business as per his forte. Both of them were still living with their god aunt who had now retired from insurance. One time on a sunny Friday afternoon, Kgosi didn't have classes and Maps decided to take him with on his adventure to the other world, making him promise not to divulge any of what he heard or saw to anyone else, not even his closest friends or family. One of Maps' major tasks was to groom someone else, as had been done with him by Phats, but from a different planet in his own galaxy—the Milky Way Galaxy. Grooming family members was against the Union's laws and thus he couldn't groom Kgosi albeit he was a good candidate. That task would have to be carried out by someone else from the Union.

A few years had lapsed since Phats *transitioned*. Maps was still frequenting the mountain top and his brother, Kgosi would accompany him on some days. It was a breezy autumn morning and the sky was flaunting a solar-eclipse. On the mountain top was Maps basking in his solitude thinking about Phats. He recalled Phats' utterances, closed his eyes and called out his name. A familiar voice encouraged him to open his eyes and he did. As he did so, there, stood his buddy with a dark purple light around his body ready to embrace Maps with the same amount of love and affection as before he passed on to the other world. The watery eyes were a sure sign of how much Maps had missed his bestie. "I'm glad you called me because there's something else that I need to share with you. The omniverse is now at a point where it doesn't necessarily need the I.G.U anymore. The wars we've fought before have all led to this point. There can no longer be any harm done to it," explained Phats. "How so?" asked Maps. Phats let out a sigh of relief and a smile and continued, "Your Earth is alive. Therefore it is metamorphosing into a complete water body. It is no longer able to host beings/entities below its own higher vibration. That is the case with the omniverse as well.

"The Union will have to be dissolved because the omniverse's residents now have a frequency that allows them to govern themselves at the highest level/vibration possible. Our elders taught us that vibration is synonymous with benevolence. You can rest now, my friend. Your task is complete." "That brings so much joy to me. I've been thinking a lot about retiring. I need to spend more time with my family. It is imperative," exclaimed Maps. The two friends shift their concentration to the eclipse and savor the moment.

BONUS CHAPTER

Life is a canvas. It is a manuscript that is never published till you give your consent.

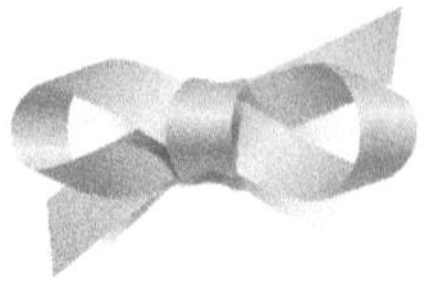

Manuscripts and Broken Promises

Zibo began to speak. "Don't you ever wonder—?"

"Here we go," interjected Asante, teasingly.

"Whatever, Asa. Seriously though, don't you ever wonder how homeless people survive the craziness that goes on in the world? For example, when there's a pandemic of some sort, they seem to be less worried about their physical health than a good meal at the end of the day. For some, it's a good smoke-or both. Here we are sanitizing our fears away while they seem unbothered-or we don't give ourselves the chance to actually see how really bothered they are.

"We, as the more "fortunate" ones frequently bump into the homeless on our way to our safe havens, sometimes looking at *them* as the loony ones. How come some of them even tend to outlive those of us with all that we have access to? Do we ever just pause for a bit and ask ourselves what manuscripts these unfortunate souls have and what promise(s) they made to themselves but were unable to keep? Are we really that much different?

"You're crazy, Zibo!"

"*I*'m crazy? You're the one who's probably going to submit our entire conversation to a publishing platform online somewhere, Asante."

"You know me too well, buddy. Especially because it's been a while since I put pen to paper!" chuckled Asante.

• • ❧ • •

ZIBO IS A PART-TIME farmer who rents out part of a family friend's farm in Orapa[1]. She owns an herb store in Phakalane[2] not far from where she stays in the village of Oodi. It has been a while since she has seen her best friend, Asante. He just returned from a writer's workshop in neighboring South Africa about a week ago. On that Wednesday after Asante got back to Botswana, he got a call from Zibo insisting on a plan that he come over to spend the day at her house the coming Saturday.

"Thank you for suggesting that I come and visit you. I really needed the outing. Plus, the ambiance at your place is truly on another level. The *vibes* are something else," gushed Asante.

"You're thanking me but I know I'm the one who's going to be grateful at the end of the day. Anyway, you're welcome, I guess," exclaimed Zibo as she handed Asante a glass of home-brewed *gemere*[4] on one hand and a *huge* slice of her famous lemon bread with a dash of cinnamon in the other-all of the ingredients from her farm.

"Your garden is not so *mini* anymore, is it, Zibo?! You have a blessed hand, friend."

"Mama taught me well, to be honest!" exclaimed Zibo.

"That, she did! What about the business? When we talked on the phone last week, you said there was a beneficial partnership that you were considering. What did you decide?"

"That deal still gives me the chills, Asante. It came at the right time and you of all people know how much work I've put in to get to this point."

"Yes, I do know. And you deserve **all** of it!"

The hours went by and time reminded these two friends why they were so close to begin with-why they had been best friends for over fifteen years. They had covered a lot of ground with their rendezvous but still had *way* more to converse about.

"My trip to SA made me think about quite a bit," recounted Asante. "I feel like the world is full of manuscripts and broken promises. It seems like *dreams* and *20-20 visions* still carry the weight of those too exhausted but dragging their feet regardless. It looks as if even though their patience is running thin, their soles (*and souls*) have too much zeal and wisdom to throw in the towel.

"And what's happening to the earth is also quite sad. Why are humans unable to get along with Mother Nature and mother Earth?"

"You're right, Asa. There's a lot going on in the world right now. It's nothing new but somehow, it always feels different experiencing it in the now, as it happens. Some people go through a lot of shit that I, personally, wouldn't blame them if they *did* decide to throw in the towel but I respect them that much more because they don't, you know!

"When it comes to Mother Nature and Earth, I've come to realize that me being unable to get along with her, could suggest that there's an internal battle inside of myself with my own femininity. Also, that this applies to both male and female, meaning I'm off balance somehow because *As Within, So Without*!"

"Exactly! It would be amazing to hear the stories of whoever wants to tell them to us. Perhaps it's still possible. Maybe we can still learn to take better care of our planet," sighed Asante.

"Perhaps this is content coming to you when it's most needed," Zibo joked.

Asante's frown turned into a smile as he let out a chuckle. "Stop giving me weird ideas, Zibo. Although, I do appreciate them a lot!

"Perhaps, it's a realization that *manuscripts* aren't just for *professional authors/authors-to-be* because *everyone* has a story to tell. And also that maybe, just maybe, a broken promise isn't as demoralizing as fragments of broken glass for as long as one is still alive."

"It's weird how deep our conversations always go, Asa. Here I am acting all surprised as if this is anything new. Quite amazing how we sort of like, bring that out in each other all the time."

Asante took a deep breath and began. "You know we're a bunch of weirdoes. *I*'m surprised you haven't come to terms with that yet, Z.

There are a lot of aspects to this conversation but let's deconstruct it at our next *private* get-together, ok? Right now, I want you to go and get ready so you can accompany me to this spoken word event I've been invited to happening in about an hour"

"And you're telling me this *now*?!" exclaimed Zibo as she rose up from her chair in anticipation of a cherry on top to a fantastic day.

• • ❧ • •

1. A mining town located in the Central District of Botswana.
2. A suburb in Botswana situated a few kilometers from the capital city Gaborone.
3. Home-brewed ginger beer.

EPILOGUE

Driving alone at night, I'm guided by the Eastern star,
Walking where there's little light, I'm guided by the Eastern star,
Tell my momma I'll be alright,
I'll always come home.
THE END.

Also by Laone J. Mangwa

Chronicles of an Unbound Traveler
Chronicles of an Unbound Traveler
Navigating The Waters Of Antiquity
The Final Frontier

Starlight
Starlight Sensations In The South
Starlight Sentiments In The South

The Great Mystery
The Great Mystery: Origins Unveiled

Standalone
Tellings From The Ethers

Watch for more at https://titansblogtoo.wordpress.com/.

About the Author

Laone J. Mangwa (Also, *LJ Mangwa*) is a Motswana *writer*, *author* and occasional *spoken word poet* from Botswana that is fascinated with how life mimics art and vice versa. Because he is passionate about creative self-expression, he has realized that finding an outlet for it is extremely important and doing so as something greater than a hobby, just as important. Thus, **all** the work he does is centered on that, as well as *collaboration* to bring that expression to fruition. As a multi-dimensional being that also regards himself as a conduit, one of the avenues he utilizes to express himself is *writing*. He writes because he can't always have conversations with himself. That gets weird to people after a while (*unfortunately*). Also because there are tales that harbor so much inspirational energy that they *choose* to implode through outward expression! Some of his works have been published in *Kalahari Review* and *IBUA Journal*. He has authored mutliple eBooks that include *Chronicles of an Unbound Traveler, Tellings from The Ethers* and *The Great Mystery*, all of which are available everywhere for digital download.

Instagram: *@lj_writes9*

Read more at https://titansblogtoo.wordpress.com/.

www.ingramcontent.com/pod-product-compliance
Lightning Source LLC
LaVergne TN
LVHW010454160826
845677LV00012B/2479
* 9 7 9 8 2 3 0 5 4 2 4 0 7 *